HANUKKAH LIGHTS

Hanukkah Lights

STORIES OF THE SEASON
FROM NPR'S ANNUAL HOLIDAY SPECIAL

Introductions by Susan Stamberg and Murray Horwitz

Illustrations by Sandra Dionisi

Published by

 **MELCHER MEDIA**

124 West 13th Street
New York, NY 10011
www.melcher.com

National Public Radio
635 Massachusetts Avenue NW
Washington, DC 20001
npr.org

Publisher: Charles Melcher
Associate Publisher: Bonnie Eldon
Editor in Chief: Duncan Bock
Editor: David E. Brown
Production Director: Andrea Hirsh
Editorial Assistant: Lindsey Stanberry

Design by Gretchen Scoble

For NPR:
Manager: Barbara Sopato
Project Manager: Barbara A. Vierow
Program Producer/Editor: Bruce Scott
Additional Contributors: Jacques Coughlin, Ben
Roe, Andy Rosenberg, Charles Thompson, Andy
Trudeau, and Alphonse Vinh
Special thanks to Susan Stamberg and Murray
Horwitz for their heartfelt introductions and
insightful contributions to the project.

Library of Congress Cataloging-in-Publication
Data

Hanukkah lights : stories of the season: from
NPR's annual holiday special / introductions by
Susan Stamberg and Murray Horwitz; illustra-
tions by Sandra Dionisi.
    p. cm.
  1. American fiction–Jewish authors. 2. Jews–
United States–Fiction. 3. Hanukkah stories. 4.
Jewish fiction. I. National Public Radio (U.S.)
  PS647.J4H36 2005
  813'.0108334–dc22
2005014453

09 08 07 06 05   10 9 8 7 6 5 4 3 2 1

Printed in China

ISBN-13 978-1-59591-009-7
ISBN-10   1-59591-009-3

Contents

Lighting the Lights for Radio and Print

By Susan Stamberg

THIS IS A BOOK FULL OF MIRACLES. OF COURSE! IT'S A COLLECTION of Hanukkah stories. And Hanukkah is all about miracles, and belief.

The book began with a radio program, which in turn led to the creation of a group of original holiday stories, and sits here now in print as a carefully gathered set of Festival of Lights tales. A curious path. No passport for that kind of trip. But hours of reading and listening pleasure.

In 1990 National Public Radio began an annual tradition: an hour-long program of stories about Hanukkah, to be broadcast during the Jewish holiday. For the first few years of the program we hunted down Hanukkah stories that had been published but rarely broadcast. Then we began commissioning stories from some of the best Jewish writers we could find. In the last twelve years or so, almost all of the stories have been written especially for us. And over these years, our list of "best Jewish writers" has grown and flourished. The authors are a mix of young and old, new and established, and their writing is humorous, compassionate, personal, reflective. These stories have filled countless radios with warmth. And, because all the stories began as literature, they are good to curl up with in a comfy armchair.

You'll smile at Anne Roiphe's hilarious account, in "The Demon Foiled," of a new Jewish mayor, lighting—or at least trying to light—the family Hanukkah candles while a local TV crew takes pictures. Mr. Mayor puts such a brilliant spin on his candle-lighting difficulties that he just might end up in the White House! And if that's not contemporary enough, Harlan Ellison (in "Go Toward the Light") and Simone Zelitch (in "The Miracle of the Oil") find in the cruse of oil that burned for eight days a link to the technology of today, and issues that occupy our daily headlines.

In "A Candle for Kerala" (on the CD that accompanies this book), Ariel Dorfman tells the story of a high-tech love that plays out in different religions and different continents. Gloria DeVidas Kirchheimer's "Nona Maccabeus" also crosses ethnic lines, again with heartwarming results. And Dani Shapiro, in "Oil and Water," gives a moving account of a family feud and reconciliation—deeply felt and so carefully observed. Shapiro's narrator visits the home of her Aunt Shirl and finds, "it is so quiet inside that you can hear all the clocks ticking."

It's even quieter than that when we record these Hanukkah stories every year at NPR. It's one of my favorite annual broadcasting journeys—going up to Studio 4-B to make the program. My recording partner, Murray Horwitz, and I wrap our voices around these heart-lifting, sad-making, laugh-inducing tales, each one different, but woven together by a continuity of religious experience. And—not the least of it—every year I have the great pleasure of being able to use, on occasion, a Yiddish accent learned, unevenly, at my father's knee. (As an NPR news correspondent I rarely get to exercise those particular chops!)

Studio 4-B is a terrific workspace. NPR's major cultural and performance programs are produced and recorded there. Unlike the NPR News studios, 4-B is serene. The lights are low. The maple floor gives the place a golden glow. You don't rush in panting, "This just in!" Instead, you kind of float through the door, adjust the microphone, clear your throat, and get ready to track. Through our headphones, producer Bruce Scott asks us to go ahead, or stop and reread a passage or two if we've stumbled or not quite gotten the emphasis. And—this is the best part—we readers listen to one another. Murray comes from a theater background and can enact all the characters in a single story. Sometimes, even though my microphone is turned off while he tracks, I have to cover my mouth so my laughter doesn't blast across to his mic and spoil his take. And when it's my turn, Murray smiles encouragement, makes suggestions, weighs in on any Hebrew pronunciations, and polishes up my Yiddish accent if Dad's lessons didn't cover a particular word. In addition to our solos, there are stories Murray and I read aloud together—typecasting: I do the women's parts. And through it all, we enjoy weaving aloud the threads of the narratives, and taking our listeners to so many different places, through the power of good fiction.

Now, in your hands, are the results of some of those sessions: the book, a collection of twelve stories, picked (with great difficulty) from some forty we've used over the years, and on the CD, four more stories, recorded by Murray and me in that serene studio where the Hanukkah candles are lit weeks before the holiday, so their glow pours out of the radio at just the right moment.

A Small Miracle Happened Here

By Murray Horwitz

IT WAS MORE OF A COMMAND THAN A SUGGESTION. JUST A FEW weeks after I had started working at NPR, the marketing director was standing in my office doorway, literally hollering: "We need more holiday specials!" Of course, it being public radio, there was no money for such things. What could we do that would be good, different, and, uh, inexpensive?

I knew from having performed a one-man show of Sholom Aleichem stories that the master had a wonderful tale about playing pinochle on Hanukkah. I figured there must be plenty more where that came from, picked up the phone, dialed Susan Stamberg, and pitched her the idea of our reading Hanukkah stories together on the radio. It is safe to say that if Susan had said no, there would have been no "Hanukkah Lights." Who else could have brought such talent and credibility—not to mention popularity—to the project?

Happily, Susan agreed at once. Senior producer Andy Trudeau assigned Bruce Scott—the son of a Methodist minister—to produce the show. And I soon learned how little I knew of my own heritage. In the first place, what I really knew about Hanukkah amounted to very little. Second, there were not loads and loads of Hanukkah stories. In fact, there were rather few. The reasons for these two circumstances may be related: Hanukkah is really a minor holiday. You won't find it in the Bible. The weekly Sabbath is of greater importance.

Yet here in the United States, Hanukkah is the most widely observed Jewish holiday after Passover and Yom Kippur. This famously has to do with the close temporal relationship of Hanukkah and Christmas. It gives Jewish families in a predominantly Christian society "our own" holiday, so that—especially as children—we don't feel "left out."

Don't get me started. But there is some legitimacy to this: Both holidays fall near the winter solstice, the darkest day of the year, and both holidays celebrate light. Hanukkah, though, is about light—the blessing of it, the necessity of it, the miracle of it.

That in itself would seem inspiration enough for literature. When you add the dramatic story—the Jews, forbidden to worship, rebelled against the Syrian emperor Antiochus, won, reclaimed the Temple in Jerusalem, worked to undo its terrible desecration and, with only one day's supply of kosher oil, enjoyed the light that miraculously lasted for eight days—you can imagine a torrent of stories, told in a range of voices and settings.

After only a couple of years, however, Bruce Scott found himself scraping the bottom of the barrel in his search for Hanukkah stories, and we decided to commission writers to fill the void. The result has been an exponential increase in the number of American Hanukkah stories. And it is Bruce who has done the bulk of the work in bringing them to you. He has found or commissioned nearly all of the stories, worked with the authors, and seen to the recordings. He edits out any mistakes, mixes in appropriate music, and finally gets the hour-long production to the NPR satellite transmission center well before the holiday. Not eight days of light, maybe, but a kind of miracle nonetheless.

"Hanukkah Lights" is now among the most successful of all NPR special programs. For that we can thank the nation's public radio stations, but mostly we need to thank the authors of these stories. When "Hanukkah Lights" began, I was a little worried about the title; I thought it sounded like a pack of cigarettes. But it turns out that each of these stories is indeed a little candle, offered with the hope that its light will stay with you long past the holiday season.

Happy Hanukkah!

Who Can Retell

By Myra Goldberg

WHEN I WAS A CHILD I LONGED TO BE HEROIC, FOR I WAS ardent, full of artistic and ethical ideas. But our household gods were Lincoln, and Einstein, and from the seriousness that surrounded them, I assumed that heroes were serious men— although the men in my family were jokers. While I was, my brother said, an easy laugh, an audience.

The Christmas of 1959 I was eleven, an age of mastery and ambition. I could bike everywhere, dance in *The Carnival of the Animals,* and play "Dark Eyes" on the violin. Surely I was destined to leave life's audience and leap, climb, or struggle into some wider, more active realm. It's possible that a similar spirit inspired the officials at the Waverly School in suburban Pelham to decree, as a new decade was about to dawn, that the eight Jews in chorus should represent our race by singing Hanukkah songs at the Christmas show. Of the eight eleven-year-olds, only Bonnie Gorelick knew the songs. But everyone was loud and full of gusto.

Who can retell the things that befell us
Who can count them
In every age a hero or sage
Came to our aid.
Ahhhhhh.

"The Waverly School Glee Club will Present a Program of Holiday songs, Thursday, December 14, 1959." I read the mimeo'd sheet to my mother, who lifted the lid of a tin pot to let the steam out.

"Of course I'll come." My mother hadn't missed a perform-ance since I played a pumpkin in Cinderella.

"Never mind, I'll be sick on Thursday," I said. "Holiday songs are boring." I loved the Christmas songs, especially "Angels We Have Heard on High," with its wide-ranging glorias. But the Jewish songs, with their tortured syntax and antiquated diction, sounded more like the patriotic hymns we usually sang at school. Maybe, as my father said, they'd lost in translation.

My mother plunged a silver fork into the pot and lifted out a giant tongue, laying it on an Early American platter. I wondered if the cow had died with its tongue curled up.

"I'm in two choruses, really, Christmas and Hanukkah. Is that fair? The other kids already know the Christmas songs." This sounded like I was against learning something, which was not a possibility in this family. "Only Bonnie knew the Hanukkah songs. From Temple." Temple, my father said, was an American invention with English services and girls getting Bar Mitzvahed.

Who can retell the things that befell us.
Who can count them,
In every age a hero or sage came to our aid.

My mother said, "We used to sing that in Hebrew, at Auntie Schulman's Hanukkah party, which Grandpa wouldn't come to, on general principles, being antisocial, and also against religion, but Grandma..." My mother began to slice the dense narrow tip of the tongue into slender pieces. "'So long as you don't say anything foolish.' That was Mama's religion."

The tongue began looking less like tongue and more like deli meat as I got drawn into my mother's story.

Grandma had carried two feather pillows, an orphan's belief in orderly anarchy, and absolute kindness from Odessa to Schenectady. She lay in a nearby hospital, dying. A priest tiptoed over, whispering to the dozing old woman, "Would you mind if I bless you?"

Grandma, still sharp-eared, pondered. Pogroms. Priests. Organized religion. Organized anything. Then the perils of hurting a real human being's feelings. "So long as you don't say anything foolish," she said, cutting a path through kindness, skepticism, aversion. She died soon after, leaving us her story.

My mother's eyes teared up and she started to hum. "Who can retell the things that befell us, who can count them."

We clasped hands, marching solemnly around the kitchen, then my mother put one hand on my waist and another on my shoulder, and we polkaed.

"Ha!" I shouted like a Cossack, then backed away. "I don't get that school. The two choruses." I stamped my foot. There was a lot I didn't get about school. At home we took a serious question and carried it around the kitchen. We danced to it, laughed to it, told stories to go with it. At school, we sat solemnly to answer foolish questions, then handed in the answers when the bell rang.

"Mom." Inspired, as my brother in his football jersey came into the kitchen, "Don't you think we should all just sing together? Sing *everything* together?" There, that sounded democratic.

"Of course you should. But it's Mr. Deanto's chorus, so do what he asks."

Mr. Deanto threw chalk at Danny Napolitano in music appreciation. He lassoed me with a violin case strap in the instrument closet and yelled, "Giddap Horsie" in a weird voice. But I never told.

My brother Michael took a step back, raising his arm to pass an imaginary football to me. "If you make a spectacle of yourself, I'll never forgive you," he said. Michael had applied to be one of the first public school Jewish kids to go to Dartmouth.

I missed the pass and crashed into his middle. "This family," he shouted, "is always making a stupid fuss about nothing."

The tongue tasted warm and salty at dinner, which was more, my father said, than you could say for the rubber chicken he'd had for lunch at the Republican fund-raiser.

"But Dad," I cried. My dad owned a picture of FDR signing the Social Security Act with a light shining over his shoulder, like St. Francis with his halo. Americans in Pelham voted Republican and were Yankee fans, but everyone else (meaning Catholics or Jews) was for Democrats and the Dodgers.

"What do you know?" he said mildly, tapping his pipe against the ashtray. "They ask, I contribute. They invite me to dinner, I go. They run the state, the state runs the Labor Department." He sounded more irritated now, in the comfortable room his labor had bought us. "They're okay as individuals. Listen to the joke I heard tonight:

"Goldberg and Smith had each boasted that they could walk on water. A crowd gathered as the two men started into the freezing waves of Coney Island. Goldberg got a few steps past the jetty, but Smith sank to his waist almost immediately. The crowd murmured. Goldberg turned around. 'On the rocks, you fool. On the rocks.'"

My father had soothed himself with the story. "The rich can afford to be rigid. The rest of us need to bend. Some things are worth sticking your neck out for. Rubber chicken and twenty-five dollars are not."

I wondered how you knew the difference. My father had stuck his neck out for the Spanish Civil War, and Workman's Compensation. At fifteen, he had traveled across Europe to America with two little brothers, to find their father on...was it Orchard? Broome? Essex Street?

I told him about the two-chorus problem.

"So," he tapped his pipe again. "They want a Jewish song. That's good."

"No, Dad. They want a Jewish song sung by Jewish kids."

"What for?"

"So *we'll* know we're Jewish?"

My father, who'd lived five miles from Auschwitz until he was fifteen, didn't think being Jewish was forgettable.

"So *they'll* know we're Jewish?" I answered my own question. "Yoo hoo, Mrs. Goldberg," I cried. This came from a television program I got teased about at school.

My father tapped *The Letters of Justice Oliver Wendell Holmes,* one of his heroes. "Every argument has an inarticulate major premise," Holmes had written.

"It's their country." I guessed the premise. "It's Deanto's chorus."

My father's face said okay, not great.

"Christmas is everybody's business. Hanukkah is only ours."

My father leaned forward slowly and shook my hand. "Whatever *should* be, you've hit the nail on the hammer of what is."

I groaned, pleased with myself. My father was a famous mangler of English clichés.

That night, the music on my favorite radio program wandered among black keys, then white, paused, joked, argued, searched itself and the keyboard for a way forward, landed somewhere else. "That," said Symphony Sid, "was ''Round Midnight,' by Thelonius Monk."

✳

The next afternoon at chorus rehearsal, I did the glorias as if I were scat singing. Then, instead of waiting to be called for "Who Can Retell," I scooted down between the chorus members until I reached Mr. Deanto.

"Please, Mr. Deanto, I'm wondering why all the students don't sing all the songs. Together." He kept staring at the chorus behind me.

That chorus was staring at me. Would Deanto throw his stick? Or wave it like a wand to send me back to chorus?

Instead, he motioned to the other Jews. "Come on down."

Micky, Arthur, Anita, Sylvia, Stan, Lennie, Bonnie climbed down from the risers. I slipped into my place in the line, Micky on one side, Anita on the other. I could feel that Micky was reserving judgment until Deanto made up his mind, but Anita, like me, was excited. My excitement came from following the line Thelonius played into action, in that foreign land called school. Hers came from me. We touched dresses.

"'Rock of Ages,'" commanded Mr. Deanto.

Children of the martyr race,
Whether free or fettered,
Wake the echoes of our song,
Where ye may be scattered.
Yours the message cheering,
That the time is nearing,
Which will see, all men free,
Tyrants disappearing.

"Are we a race," I whispered to Anita as everyone else repeated the last two lines.

"It says so in the song, doesn't it?"

Heady with being heard, I fanned my hand to mean maybe yes, maybe no, the way they did on TV to be Jewish. Deanto looked up at me, but I couldn't read his expression.

"Again." Deanto picked up the tempo.

What next? Anne Frank (I remembered) believed that people were good at heart. I looked directly at Deanto and when the singing died out raised my hand.

"Once more," said Deanto. "Faster."

Faster we sang. Deanto's white tipped baton waved wildly as if to signal that he'd never acknowledge me or my question. "Second verse, 'Who Can Retell.'"

I nudged Micky, but he stared straight ahead, refusing me in his strict valedictorian's way. Anita and I were alone, invisible, unhearable girls, who'd played Grandma Meets Her Man in Anita's pine-paneled basement just last week.

I turned to her, to the routine. "Yer densing?"

"Yer esking?" She rose on tiptoe, placing a hand at my waist and one on my shoulder.

"I'm esking, yer densing." I waltzed us 'round once in a clunky, caricatured way, then we ran to the edge of the stage and down into the auditorium, giggling, intoxicated, afraid in our boldness. We looked up. The red robed Hanukkah chorus was grinning, or trying not to grin, behind Deanto's navy blue back.

"Yer densing?" I lifted both hands, elegant this time.

✳

"Yer esking?" She bowed. We waltzed. We stopped. We clapped our hands above our heads like castanets. We ran up the auditorium aisle to where Enter to Learn, Leave to Serve was written above the doors. Still giggling, we pushed through the Boy's Door, which locked behind us, leaving us coatless, triumphant, outside, in the new snow of the beginning of the nineteen sixties.

Hanukkah in Chicago

By Daniel Pinkwater

ONE DAY—IT SEEMED LIKE THE DAY BEFORE, AND ALSO A long time ago—the world was not much bigger than the apartment, the park, the backyard. His mother was with him almost all the time, or his big sister. Someone was always nearby, watching. If he was frightened, or hurt himself, if he cried, someone would be there to comfort him, and protect him.

Another day, and he was a person with business of his own, friends and enemies, a desk where he sat each school day, a teacher, books which he was not to lose, not to tear, not to allow to get dirty.

For a while, his mother or sister walked with him to the school. Later, he was allowed to walk with older children who had been strictly charged to stay with him and hold his hand, make sure he obeyed the patrol boys, big, serious eighth-graders, who stood guard at the two streets he would cross by himself. For a time, the older children held his hand all the way to school. Now the weather had turned cold. The older children still accepted the dime from his mother, but only held his hand until they reached the corner of Roscoe Street, turning south on Broadway at the hardware store, where he had once accidentally dropped a curtain rod into the hot-air register, a shiny metal grille set into the unpainted wooden floor. Once past the hardware store, the older children let go of his hand, and raced ahead. He was on his own, but he knew the way.

First he passed Mr. Graf's grocery store, where his big brother worked after school. Mr. Graf had a white shirt and a white apron, and a yellow pencil behind his ear. When his brother worked there, he put a pencil behind his ear too. The boy would see Mr. Graf through the window, watching the children on their way to school, and wave to him.

Next to Mr. Graf's grocery store was the poultry market. Often, in the morning, there would be a truck parked outside the poultry market, and men would carry crates, with wire sides, like cages, to a little window close to the sidewalk, and send them down a long metal slide into the basement. There were chickens in the crates. They were turned loose in the basement, where there was an electric light. The boy could look down through the little window and see the chickens milling about. They were beautiful with red combs and wattles, and amazing yellow feet, and the smell of living chickens. He liked the speckled ones best. He always stopped for a while at the poultry market.

He also liked the fish store, dark and wet and salty-smelling, with the fish posing on an ocean of cracked ice, staring lidlessly.

His teacher was Mrs. Herman. She was sometimes like a chicken, and sometimes like a fish. She was not like his mother or his sister or his aunts. Mrs. Herman was strict. She never smiled. She knew a lot. She could teach people how to read. But it was important to be careful how one behaved, because she was strict. The boy had made some mistakes at first, and Mrs. Herman had shown how strict she could be. If someone was inappropriate, Mrs. Herman made that person wear a baby bonnet. She had a box of baby bonnets. The first thing to remember was to avoid being inappropriate.

Mrs. Herman held the key to the door through which the children entered a world that was not Chicago. It was the book about Dick and Jane, and their dog, Spot. They did not live surrounded by brick and cement. The trees were not spindly mimosas growing out of concrete in alleys and apartment house backyards. They lived among white houses and green grass.

See...the...ball. See...the...red...ball. See...the...boy...run. See...Spot...run. The children moved their lips, and their fingers beneath the words, and marveled.

There were a lot of children in the class, children from all over the neighborhood. There had just been a war, and some of the children were refugees, and did not speak our language. Some of the children who were refugees shuffled when they walked, and hardly spoke at all, or whispered. Some of them were inappropriate.

After school was over, the boy crossed Broadway, and walked up Melrose Street to the heder. He had been led there by the hand a few weeks earlier, when school had begun. The heder was another sort of school. Downstairs was the synagogue. Up a creaky stairway was the heder.

Men in black suits sat in small rooms with boys. The boys had a book. Not like Dick and Jane. The book had thick and thin letters. There were no pictures. And the letter had sounds, but no meaning. Small marks were printed under the letters, and the marks made different sounds. The boys read aloud, all together, led by the men.

Ah…aw…eh. Bah…baw…beh. Gah…gaw…geh. Dah…daw… deh. It meant nothing.

The men were strict, far more strict than Mrs. Herman.

It would be getting dark and cold when the boy walked home from the heder. An older boy was supposed to hold him by the hand, but, of course, he didn't.

It had already snowed three or four times, when things changed in Mrs. Herman's classroom. The children were allowed to cut out paper snowflakes with the little blunt scissors. The snowflakes were taped to the windows. Long ribbons of stretchy red and green paper were hung over the blackboards. And Mrs. Herman taught the children a song about Santa Claus.

Colored printed cutouts of Santa Claus were pinned to the walls. Santa Claus flew through the air, and brought children presents. Mrs. Herman brought cookies to school in a metal box with red flowers on it, and each child was given cookies to eat at his desk, and a paper napkin, with green leaves and red flowers. All the children in the school were marched to the auditorium, where they were shown cartoons, and sang songs about snow and Santa Claus. When the children came back to the classroom, there was a printed card with pictures of something that looked like Dick and Jane's house in the snow on each desk. Mrs. Herman had written the name of the child, and her name on every card.

In the heder, all the boys were made to sit at a long table, and the rabbi, who was more strict than Mrs. Herman, taught them songs. The boys had no idea what the songs were about. The men who taught the boys to read the Hebrew letters sang in loud voices, and beat on the table.

At home, the boy asked his father if Santa Claus was coming to their house.

"No, Santa Claus does not come here, but tonight we go to Uncle Dave's house."

"Does Santa Claus come to Uncle Dave's house?"

"Not Santa Claus, but just as good. You'll see."

All the uncles were there, and all the aunts, all the cousins. Everybody smelled good. The house smelled good, smells that made the boy hungry. Uncle Jack was there, who always laughed, and called the boy "Captain." The aunts kissed him and hugged him. The grown-ups hugged and kissed each other, and shook hands. They stood in the living room, and lit some candles, and sang a song.

Everyone sat at a long table, covered by a white tablecloth. There were candles on the table. Everything looked good, and sparkled in the candlelight. Aunt Sarah brought food to the table.

When each dish was brought, the grown-ups would shout, "Ahh!" and clap their hands. They would tell Aunt Sarah she was a wonderful cook. She would smile, and her face would shine in the candlelight.

There were more different things to eat than the boy had ever seen at one time. The grown-ups told jokes and laughed while everyone ate. Then, they all sat back in their chairs, and sang songs, which the boy had never seen grown-ups do.

The uncles sat in the living room, and smoked cigars and drank schnapps. The aunts were laughing and talking in the kitchen. The children played with dreidels, which were things that spin. And each uncle gave the boy a quarter. The aunts gave him handkerchiefs, and socks, and a book, with pictures, about the Jewish people, that he was almost able to read.

The grown-ups talked and listened to music on the radio. For a while, they danced. Most of the children curled up on Aunt Sarah's soft carpet and fell asleep. The boy dreamed of snow falling on Dick and Jane's house.

Stabbing an Elephant

By Max Apple

WHEN MR. JACOBSON TOOK OFF HIS SNOWY OVERCOAT
and told me "we" had a problem, I thought he spoke of the marital we.

"Should I speak to Mrs. Jacobson as well?" I asked.

"No," he said, "my wife and I are in complete agreement. This is the problem, Rabbi."

He handed me a thin blue booklet, "The Story of Hanukkah," written and illustrated by Zvi Herman. "Look at page six," he ordered.

I saw a colorful illustration—an ancient soldier wearing leather headgear and sandals jabbed his short sword into an elephant's belly. Although the elephant's knees buckled, the animal seemed otherwise undisturbed. The soldier looked up at the beast as casually as a mechanic examines a Buick on the rack.

"This is giving my child nightmares," Mr. Jacobson said. "Should a four-year-old be exposed to this, especially in a religious school environment?"

"War is awful," I agreed, "the children understand that Eleazar, Judah Maccabee's brother, is a hero defending his people and his faith."

"Rabbi," Mr. Jacobson said, "I'm talking about the elephant, not the man."

"But the story is about the man, the elephant is just a tank in a war story."

"You don't have to explain that to me—I'm talking about a four-year-old, a four-year-old who loves elephants and is inconsolable."

"I'm sorry," I said, "I had no idea. This seems so tame compared to cartoons."

"Beth doesn't watch cartoons," Mr. Jacobson said. "She sleeps with Babar in one hand and his wife, Chelsea, in the other. After her fourth birthday she asked us to send all her presents to an African game reserve for the elephants."

"A remarkable child," I said.

"She is," Mr. Jacobson said. "As you can see I married late in life...what I'm learning from her...it chokes me up, Rabbi...this child is so precious to me."

"Of course," I said, "I feel terrible about this. If it's okay with you, I'll come to your home tonight to speak with Beth."

"What will you tell her?"

"Maybe we'll talk about the candles rather than the war."

Mr. Jacobson shook his head. "Not tonight, we're having a consultation with Bill Hazelton, the head of psychiatry at the med school. You may know that Helen, my wife, is a psychotherapist.

She told Bill what's been going on and he's seeing Beth tonight as a professional favor. I don't think Beth needs a psychiatrist and a rabbi in one evening."

I agreed.

"But it's an important matter," he said. "In the last two days Beth has regressed six months."

"Does that put her back to Passover?" I quipped.

"It puts her back to diapers," Mr. Jacobson said. "This is not a joking matter. Beth is at a crucial developmental stage. Her value system is under attack. She's been taught that the Jewish soldiers are good and she knows without teaching that elephants are good. Can you understand the dilemma?

"I'll call you in the morning, Rabbi," he said, "to discuss Dr. Hazelton's recommendations."

This was the biggest crisis of my brief career as a rabbi. Harold Solomon, my immediate predecessor at Temple Emanuel, now had a small congregation in Atlanta. In spite of rumors about him and several married women, he was enormously popular. After six years he grew weary of waiting for Rabbi Edwards to retire.

I benefited from his impatience. In this, only my second year, Rabbi Edwards announced his retirement. He did so from the pulpit on Rosh Hashanah.

"Beginning next Friday evening," he said—then he paused. He was the master of the dramatic pause. This time he surprised the entire congregation. "Next Friday evening and thereafter...I am going to share the pulpit on a biweekly basis with my distinguished junior colleague, Rabbi Wohlman."

Everyone knew what that meant. He had selected me to succeed him. Rabbi Solomon's fans, mostly the young marrieds and
the singles, were not happy.

They plotted. The board held a meeting but my supporters
prevailed. Dr. Firestone, an orthopedic surgeon, the current
president, met with me.

"You know that Rabbi Solomon had great rapport with much
of the congregation. Every summer he led a young couples'
adventure tour."

"I've heard him praised," I said.

"I told his fans," Dr. Firestone said, "that we needed a rabbi,
not a tour guide, but you might think about taking a group somewhere. The only criticism I heard was that you're not as adventurous as Rabbi Solomon."

"There were no classes in adventure at the seminary," I said.

Dr. Firestone smiled. "That's a relief," he said, "but you know
what I'm getting at, people liked Harold because they say he didn't
act like a rabbi—I'm just passing that on for what it's worth."

"I'll keep it in mind," I said, and I did; only I wasn't sure how
not to act. Adventure seemed easier. I contacted a travel agency
that specialized in it. I could lead a prayer service in the Amazon,
along the Urubumba River, or while ballooning in New Zealand,
each at about the same price. I chose the Amazon thinking it
would be a relief from snowy Detroit. Thus far, no congregants
had reserved a space, but there was still plenty of time.

In the morning just before Mr. Jacobson called, Jane Kaplan, a young divorcée who had gone on Rabbi Solomon's Urubumba trip, stopped to criticize my selection.

"We've been to South America," she said. "Why not try another continent?"

Her blue body stocking indicated that she was either coming from or going to aerobic dancing. Even in my office she twitched. There had been rumors about her and Rabbi Solomon, but I tried to drive slander from my thoughts.

"Not everyone has been there," I said, "but I'm glad you're giving me feedback. You're the first to respond."

She looked around my small office as if she might find something on the walls beyond my degrees and photos of my brother's children.

"There used to be a photograph of Harold and the entire group in rubber suits. It was hilarious."

From the look in her eyes I knew that no matter what trip I might propose, I would never be her rabbi.

She was still in the room when Mr. Jacobson called to say that Dr. Hazelton thought a retraction would be necessary.

"Retract what?" I asked.

"The elephant," he said. "Tell the children that this event never happened, that the illustration was a mistake."

For what happened next I have no good explanation, only a theory. Until this point, Mr. Jacobson and I had not been having a dispute. I had no vested interest in the Book of the Maccabees, One or Two, and I certainly wanted to make Beth feel better. But the word "retract" stung me. Maybe it was his imperial manner or the challenge to my authority—whatever. No doubt, Jane Kaplan, standing at the doorway listening, didn't help. All this roused what the rabbis called the *Yetzer Hara,* loosely translated as "evil impulse."

"No," I told him, "I can't change the story. The elephant is a recorded fact; it's history. I can't interpret it away."

Mr. Jacobson reacted as if I had lashed him with a whip. His neck snapped.

"I've told you how much this means to my child…how much she and her mother and I are in distress over this and you refuse to make a simple retraction?"

"I have no authority to do so," I said.

"We'll see," Mr. Jacobson said.

II

When Dr. Firestone got in touch with me a few hours later, I forgot about Hanukkah. The specific charge was child abuse.

"Believe me, I hate to tell you this," Dr. Firestone said.

"I never touched the child. You know that, Mr. Jacobson knows it, Beth knows it."

"Of course you didn't. It's a legal term. Jacobson is a lawyer—he used a legal term. I'm sorry, but I had no choice. I called for an emergency board meeting tonight at 7:30. We want you to have a chance to tell your side of the story."

I went immediately to Rabbi Edwards's study.

"You want my advice?"

"Of course," I said.

Rabbi Edwards had a full head of silver hair and enunciated every syllable.

"Cut the elephant; it's apocrypha not Torah."

"It doesn't seem right," I said. "It's the one detail that always made the story seem real to me."

"Who's gonna care?" Rabbi Edwards asked, "ten four-year-olds? Look, I've known Sy Jacobson for twenty-five years. Sure he's a little nuts about his kid. He was a bachelor until he was forty-eight. I can't tell you how many times women called me to ask about him when he was president of the temple. I told them all, 'I'm a rabbi, not a marriage broker.' I thought he was gay myself. Then one day he called, told me he was in love and that was it. They got married right here in the study."

"So you would do it because he's your friend?"

"I would do it," Rabbi Edwards said, "because you're running a nursery school, not the Sanhedrin. If you're going to succeed with this or any congregation you'll have to learn to take your stand on things that matter, otherwise you'll throw away all the good will you have. Good will, that's a rabbi's capital. Waste it and it's gone forever."

"Will you be at the board meeting?" I asked.

He shook his head. "I'll be in Orlando for the Interfaith Council meeting. I'm leaving in an hour." He put an experienced hand on my shoulder. "God tests us all," he said, "but this, this isn't from God, it's from Sesame Street. Settle it quickly."

I knew, as I walked along the deserted school corridor, that I had two clear choices. I could retract the elephant, or like Judah Maccabee's brother, let it crush me.

From the window of my school office I saw a Yellow Cab come for Rabbi Edwards. I watched Detroit darken and my Honda Accord begin to disappear beneath soft thick snow. The secretary saying good-bye startled me at five. Alone in the empty building, I opened Maccabees One. The elephant was there. I could almost see him—not Babar, but a big gray tusk-heavy bull bearing down on the Jewish people. I watched the battle unfold as if it was an adventure movie. Judah and his brothers had seen the temple desecrated, the pious destroyed, and in a line that startled me, I read that even the beauty of the Hebrew women had been altered.

Not one elephant, but thirty-two marched against the Maccabees, and Eleazar, the elephant slayer, did not resemble his warrior brother. Perhaps because of the illustration in Beth's book, I imagined him thin, sandals and headgear a size too large.

The elephants had been fed grape and mulberry juice to enrage them. On their backs, in bucket seats, each beast carried four powerful men. The noise of this army marching from Antioch clogged Eleazar's ears. The sun bouncing from their brass shields lighted the mountains. He choked on the dust—his comrades who had fought for a generation fled before these machines of destruction, and then, this modest man, this overlooked brother—something happened to him. He stepped forward, out of himself into history. Far be it from me to remove him.

When I closed the book it was 7:20 and my heart was pounding. With two fingers, on the typewriter Rabbi Solomon had left behind, I wrote my letter of resignation. I had just finished when Beth's preschool teacher, Julie, knocked and then entered. I had instructed Julie last year in conversion class, and had been seeing her socially, less regularly than she wished, but I told her that I wanted to solidify my career before making larger plans.

"Why are you doing this?" she asked. "Why are you throwing away your career over an elephant?"

At that moment, fired by the story, I felt heroic myself—also strongly attracted to Julie. Her concern showed. Like the women in the text her beauty had been altered by struggle, to me heightened. I wanted to embrace her, but in the hallway I heard the eight board members.

"I appreciate your concern," I said. "I'm trying to do what a rabbi should do."

"I don't understand you," she said, "to give the jerks what they want you're willing to take a tour group to the Amazon, but to keep a sweet little girl from having nightmares you won't retract an elephant."

"I can't," I said. "The elephant is history, the jerks aren't."

"You know they'll fire you, don't you? Sy Jacobson has the board in his pocket. He's a past president and an important lawyer and his wife is on TV all the time. You can't fight them."

"I'm not fighting anybody," I said. "I'm making a rabbinical decision."

Ten minutes later I said the same thing to the board. Julie was in the room with the eight temple trustees, so was Mr. Jacobson. As in court, I sat across the room from my accuser. In the hallway

Beth, clutching Babar dressed in a green vest, waited with her Latin American baby-sitter.

"First," I said, "I regret whatever anxiety I have brought to Beth. This concerns me more than anything else. But if I set a precedent here, what will I tell a parent whose child loves rams when he or she comes to me next September demanding the ram be omitted from the story of the sacrifice of Isaac. To please that child, should I let Abraham kill his son?"

"We're talking about an elephant, not a ram," Mr. Jacobson said. "We're talking about a specific child, not a theoretical one. Don't confuse the issue."

"May I invite Beth in?" I asked Mr. Jacobson.

"Yes," he said. "She wants to be here—to see justice done."

I faced the lawyer, the teacher, and the child. I had King Solomon's example before me, also Rabbi Solomon's. King Solomon would have ferreted out the true solution; Rabbi Solomon would have taken the child to an elephant love-in in Thailand. I had neither the wisdom of old Solomon nor the adventurous spirit of young Solomon. I had a sweet child before me, a father who would turn the world upside-down for her, and a teacher who understood elephants, but not rabbis.

"I want to correct one thing in the book," I told Beth. "What really happened was slightly different. In those days people usually rode on camels. The soldier killed a camel, not an elephant, and he was very sad about that, but he had to do it."

Mr. Jacobson gave me a suspicious look, then waited for Beth. Dr. Firestone and the board both waited. Julie waited. Beth, in a strong voice, decided.

"You can't change an elephant to a camel."

Jacobson smiled, proud of his daughter's cleverness. I handed my letter of resignation to Dr. Firestone.

Julie crouched on her knees—eye level to the child.

"Beth," she said, "you know I wasn't born Jewish. I changed. And how do you think that happened?"

Beth shook her head, she didn't seem to care.

"I had to really want to do it, and it wasn't easy," Julie said. "If people can change, why can't elephants?"

Beth hesitated, considering the possibility. She looked at me and I saw beneath her trimmed bangs eyes that had studied species variation in *Where the Wild Things Are.*

She shifted her weight, causing her father's swivel chair to move as she looked at him for advice.

Mr. Jacobson said nothing. Julie still crouching beside Beth made the case silently for the camel and all other converts.

"Are you going to change again?" Beth asked her teacher.

"I can answer that," I said. "Julie's not going to change, but I am."

Before the child made up her mind, I did. In front of the assembled board, I took my first adventure trip—across the room to Julie.

"I guess it's OK," Beth said, in a quiet voice that I hardly heard.

I reached for Julie's hand, but her pupil, quickened by relief, jumped from her father's lap and beat me to it.

✳

Nona Maccabeus

By Gloria DeVidas Kirchheimer

SOMEONE HAD THE BRIGHT IDEA THAT THE RESIDENTS OF the Coney Island Sephardic Home would enjoy some entertainment on the first night of Hanukkah. The social director was ecstatic. She wore her wig as though it was a crown of office. My grandmother laughed at her behind her back. "*No sabé nada*—She doesn't know anything," she said to me when I came for my weekly visit. "But Nona," I said, "she went to school, she knows all about working in a place like this." Mrs. Steinberg's Ph.D. meant nothing to my grandmother.

Nona, who was never taught to read as a girl in Izmir, Turkey, was proud of my grandfather, a lay rabbi, because he knew how to read.

"And so do I, Nona."

She took her hand and put it on my stomach. "Reading can

make a woman crazy," she said. "All you need to read are the signs and wonders. They will tell you to be fruitful and multiply. Ayyy, your grandfather was the light of my eyes—*la luz de mis ojos.*" We were speaking in Ladino, the medieval Spanish we carried with us from Spain after the Inquisition and into the Ottoman Empire. Nona had taught me many proverbs and songs. She was humming one now, as she rocked on the veranda.

The Coney Island Sephardic Home faced the boardwalk and the Parachute Jump. It was a warm day for December and the smell of cotton candy wafted over us. But most importantly, one could smell the sea breezes which were known to have curative powers. I held Nona's hand as she urged me to breathe. Our respirations were interrupted by the arrival of Mrs. Steinberg—or Doctor, as she preferred to be called. She smiled at me and said to Nona, *"A shayna maidel."*

Dr. Steinberg had not yet caught on to the fact that the majority of the residents of the Home were Sephardic and not Ashkenazi like her, and could not understand Yiddish. Spanish, yes. Greek, Arabic, Turkish, French, Armenian—certainly. Nona wagged her finger at the woman and quoted a proverb in Ladino, to the effect that a closed mouth will keep out flies.

"Thanks, sweetie," the social director said to my ninety-year-old grandmother. "You be good now."

"They call her 'Doctor,'" Nona said scornfully. "Where is her white jacket?" I knew that my grandmother had no faith in doctors, white jackets notwithstanding, and relied on a string of garlic tied around her waist to ward off the evil eye. I suspected from

the telltale ridge around her middle that she was even now wearing such a belt. How she managed to procure enough garlic for
the purpose was a mystery. She did hint that she was on excellent
terms with the Hispanic kitchen workers who would have had no
difficulty understanding her. To them she complained incessantly
about the food. How she longed for some *borekas, fritadas, biscochos*—
good Sephardic home cooking. She blessed me when I finally
learned how to make some of these dishes and brought her samples
to taste.

Seeing Nona slipping into a doze, I caught up with the social
director. I heard, I said, that there will be some entertainment
next week for Hanukkah.

Dr. Steinberg clasped her hands in devotion. The granddaughter of the president of the board of directors had offered to
bring her little group of musicians to perform. They would do so
at no charge.

I asked if she had met them or perhaps heard a tape.

Steinberg's hand flew to her mouth in horror. "Oh I couldn't
do that," she said. "It would be an insult to Mr. Bensignor" (the
head of the board). I understood her position. The Home was
dependent on rich donors and he was number one.

"But why have entertainment at all?" I asked.

"Everyone likes a Hanukkah party," she said defensively.
"When I was a child we had what we called a Hanukkah bush. And
the kids got a present for each of the eight days." For a moment I
was retroactively envious. As a Sephardic little girl, I had to be
content with only one present for the holiday. "Also," Dr.

✦

Steinberg continued, "we can't have a repeat of what happened last year."

The previous social director had presided over last year's Hanukkah and was fired immediately afterward.

What happened was this. On the first night, each resident brought a menorah to the lounge. These were set on a long table and one by one, they were lit by their owners. Just as the last candle was lit, one resident, a Mr. Matalon, seized his menorah, a handsome weighty silver object that had been in his family for generations, and refused to leave it with the others. Following the letter of the law, he was going to take it to his room and set it in the window so it could be seen by passers-by. ("We have those mesh curtains in every room, you can imagine…" said Dr. Steinberg.) A wrestling match ensued during which two attendants were summoned to pry the elderly man's hands from his heirloom. In the course of the struggle, the menorah fell down and ignited the corner of a tablecloth. "Thank goodness it was only the first night," Dr. Steinberg said, "one candle plus the shamas. I was called in to interview for the social director's job the next day."

I could see why she would want to erase the memory of last year's event with some entertainment.

When I arrived at the Home a week later along with other relatives for the first night of Hanukkah, there didn't seem to be any evidence of an incipient conflagration. (Mr. Matalon, last year's firebrand, had rejoined his ancestors.) People were already beginning to step up to the large table where all the candelabra had been set, each with a nametag to avoid controversy. Every resident was invited to light a candle on his or her own menorah with the assistance of an aide or a relative. Nona's hand was surprisingly steady and she brushed me away when I offered to help.

Dr. Steinberg kept glancing at the door to the lounge. Where were the entertainers? Was she going to have to come up with an alternative to what had been scheduled?

"When do we eat?" the aristocratic Mr. Abravanel said, banging on the ground with his cane. Great tufts of hair sprouted from his ears which at this point in his life were purely ornamental since he was stone deaf and refused to wear a hearing aid.

"Quick," Nona whispered to me, "give me the *lokmas* you brought before he steals them." She started to pat me down, looking for this culinary treat, the Sephardic equivalent of latkes. Fortunately, at that moment the door burst open and a troupe of young people came hurrying in, laughing. The musicians, at last.

And here is what the elderly residents saw: a couple of young women with bare midriffs despite the December weather, one of them sporting a twinkling belly button and tattoos up her arms, the other wearing a nose ring. Then there was a boy with one earring and a shaved head, wearing tight black leather; another had dreadlocks, while the remaining boys, or maybe they were girls, were wearing scruffy sneakers and T-shirts. One of them had a large black hat on, the kind worn by some Hasidim. They carried a motley range of instruments.

With an agonized smile, Dr. Steinberg introduced the leader, Dawn Bensignor, who began by saying, "Like—this is so not us, being late and all, but the van…" She trailed off. The audience was getting restless. There was a lot of murmuring. A woman called out in Ladino, "*Que verguenza!*—Shame on you!"

"Okay, guys" Dawn said, "here's our hip-hop Hanukkah."

Sound blasted out of the electric guitar while a bongo kept the beat. There was actually an oud, an ancient Middle Eastern instrument making noises never anticipated by the shepherds of Anatolia. The music seemed to be a cross between Israeli rock and Times Square subway music, particularly the kind you hear when you switch from the Number One train to the BMT. I half expected the writhing of one of the musicians to turn into a break dance.

The audience applauded politely at the end of each number, but some of the women were tittering. I noticed that my grand-mother had disappeared but her cane was under her chair, which meant she intended to return.

"Now what about a sing-along," Ms. Bensignor suggested.

Just then my grandmother appeared in the doorway, resplen-dent in a white silk outfit shot with gold and silver filigree. There were tassels at her wrists and at the hem of the garment. A fringe of gold coins hung from a silk cap over her forehead. In her hand she held a tambourine. She raised it high and gave it a shake. The band whooped with delight. Everyone started clapping and shouting as though awakened from a stupor. In a quavering voice Nona began singing a Hanukkah song in Ladino that I remem-bered from my childhood, and this time everyone joined in.

Later, while helping Nona get out of her costume, which must have been over a hundred years old, I congratulated her on her performance.

"I did it for your grandfather of blessed memory. He was the light of my eyes," she said again to me. "The light of the candles reminds me of him."

She folded up the silk costume carefully—the vest, the balloon pants, the sash, the open caftan with its exquisite embroidery. "Now it's yours," she said.

"But Nona," I said, "maybe next year...?"

She shook her head. I kissed her and promised to come back soon.

Though she didn't realize it, my grandmother had penetrated the significance of Hanukkah. Aside from the consecrated oil—the candles—that burned for eight days, Hanukkah was the victory of the Jews against their Hellenistic-Syrian oppressors. In her own way Nona was the spiritual descendant of the Maccabees who didn't give in to an alien culture. She was not going to be taken over—not by the Ashkenazim who controlled her daily activities, nor by the current youth culture. I think of her victory every time I light the candles.

✳

Go Toward the Light

By Harlan Ellison

IT WAS A TIME OF MIRACLES.

Time, itself, was the first miracle. That we had learned how to drift backward through it, that we had been able to achieve it at all: another miracle. And the most remarkably miraculous miracle of all: that of the one hundred and sixty-five physicists, linguists, philologists, archaeologists, engineers, technicians, programmers of large-scale numerical simulations, and historians who worked on the Timedrift Project, only two were Jews. Me, myself, Matty Simon, a timedrifter, what is technically referred to on my monthly paycheck as an authentic "chronocircumnavigator"— euphemistically called a "fugitive" by the one hundred and sixty-three Gentile techno-freaks and computer jockeys—short-speak for *Tempus Fugit*—"Time Flies"—broken-backed Latin, just a "fugitive." That's me, young Matty, and the other Jew is Barry Levin.

Not Le*vine* and not Le*veen*, but Levin, as if to rhyme with "let me in." Mr. Barry R. Levin, Fields Medal nominee, post-adolescent genius and wiseguy, the young man who Stephen Hawking (yeah, courtesy of the over-the-counter anti-agathic drugs, still alive, and breaking a hundred on the links) says has made the greatest contributions to quantum gravity, the guy who, if you ask him a simple question you get a pageant, endless lectures on chrono-string theory, complexity theory, algebraic number theory, how many pepperonis can dance on the point of a pizza. Also, Barry Levin, orthodox Jew. Did I say *orthodox*? Beyond, galactically *beyond* orthodox. So damned orthodox that, by comparison, Moses was a *fresser* of barbequed pork sandwiches with Texas hot links. Levin, who was *frum,* Chassid, a reader and quoter of the Talmud, and also the biggest pain in the…I am a scientist, I am not allowed to use that kind of language. A pain in the nadir, the fundament, the buttocks, the *tuchis*!

A man who drove everyone crazy on Project Timedrift by continuing to insist: while it is all well and good to be going back to record at first hand every aspect of the Greek Culture, nonetheless, the Hellenic World was enriched and enlightened by the Israelites and so, by rights, we ought to be making book on the parallel history of the Jews.

With one hundred and sixty-three *goyim* on the Project, you can imagine with what admiration and glee this unending assertion was received. Gratefully, we were working out of the University of Chicago, and not Pinsk, so at least I didn't have to worry about pogroms.

*

What I *did* worry about was Levin's characterization of me as a "pretend Jew."

"You're not a Good Jew," he said to me yesterday. We were lying side by side in the REM sleep room, relaxing after a three-hour hypnosleep session learning the idiomatics of Ptolemaic Egyptian, all ninety-seven dialects. He in his sling, me in mine. "I *beg* your sanctimonious pardon," I said angrily. "And you, I suppose, are a *Good* Jew, by comparison to my being a *Bad* Jew!"

"*Res ipsa loquitur,*" he replied, not even opening his eyes. It was Latin, and it meant *the thing speaks for itself;* it was self-evident.

"When I was fourteen years old," I said, propping myself on one elbow and looking across at him lying there with his eyes shut, "a kid named Jack Wheeldon, sitting behind me in an assembly at my junior high school, kicked my seat and called me a kike. I turned around and hit him in the head with my geography book. He was on the football team, and he broke my jaw. Don't tell me I'm a Bad Jew. I ate through a straw for three months."

He turned his head and gave me that green-eyed lizard-on-a-rock stare. "This is a Good Jew, eh? Hanukkah is in three days. You'll be lighting the candles, am I correct? You'll be reciting the prayers? You'll observe *yontiff* using nothing but virgin olive oil in your menorah, to celebrate the miracle?"

Oh, how I wanted to pop him one. "I gotcher miracle," I said, rudely. I lay back in the sling and closed my eyes.

I didn't believe in miracles. How Yehudah of the Maccabees had fielded a mere ten thousand Jews against Syrian King Antiochus's mercenary army of 60,000 infantry and 5,000 cavalry; and how he had whipped them like a tub of butter. How the victors had then marched on Jerusalem and retaken the Second Temple; and how they found that in the three years of Hellenist and Syrian domination and looting the Temple had grown desolate and overgrown with vegetation, the gates burned, and the Altar desecrated. But worst of all, the sacred vessels, including the menorah, had been stolen. So the priests, the *Kohanim,* took seven iron spits, covered them with wood, and crafted them into a makeshift menorah. But where could they find uncontaminated oil required for the lighting of the candelabrum?

It was a time of miracles. They found one flask of oil. A *cruse* of oil, whatever a cruse was. And when they lit it, a miracle transpired, or so I was told in Sunday School, which was a weird name for it because Friday sundown to Saturday sundown is the Sabbath for Jews, except we were Reform, and that meant Saturday afternoon was football and maybe a movie matinee, so I went on Sundays. And, miracle of miracles, I forgot most of those football games, but I remembered what I'd been taught about the "miracle" of the oil, if you believe that sort of mythology they tell to kids. The oil, just barely enough for one day, burned for *eight* days, giving the *Kohanim* sufficient time to prepare and receive fresh uncontaminated oil that was fit for the menorah.

A time of miracles. Like, for instance, you're on the Interstate, seventy-five miles from the nearest gas station, and your tank is empty. But you ride the fumes seventy-five miles to a fill-up. Sure. And one day's oil burns for eight. Not in *this* universe, it doesn't.

※

"I don't believe in old wives' tales that there's a 'miracle' in one day's oil burning for eight," I said.

And *he* said: "That wasn't the miracle."

And *I* said: "Seems pretty miraculous to me. If you believe."

And *he* said: "The miracle was that they knew the oil was uncontaminated. Otherwise they couldn't use it for the ceremony."

"So how did they know?" I asked.

"They found one cruse, buried in the dirt of the looted and defiled Temple of the Mount. One cruse that had been sealed with the seal of the high rabbi, the *Kohane Gadol,* the Great Priest."

"Yeah, so what's the big deal? It had the rabbi's seal on it. What did they expect, the Good Housekeeping Seal of Approval?"

"It was never done. It wasn't required that oil flasks be sealed. And rules were rigid in those days. No exceptions. No variations. Certainly the personal involvement of the *Kohane Gadol* in what was almost an act of housekeeping...well...it was unheard of. Unthinkable. Not that the High Priest would consider the task beneath him," he rushed to interject, "but it would never fall to his office. It would be considered *unworthy* of his attention."

"Heaven forfend," I said, wishing he'd get to the punchline.

Which he did. "Not only was the flask found, its seal was unbroken, indicating that the contents had not been tampered with. One miraculous cruse, clearly marked for use in defiance of all logic, tradition, random chance. And *that* was the miracle."

I chuckled. "Mystery, maybe. Miracle? I don't think so."

"Naturally you don't think so. You're a Bad Jew."

And *that,* because he was an arrogant little creep, because *his* subjective world-view was the *only* world-view, because he fried my frijoles, ranked me, dissed me, ground my gears, and in general cheesed me off...I decided to go "fugitive" and solve his damned mystery, just to slap him in his snotty face with a dead fish! When they ask you why any great and momentous event in history took place, tell 'em that all the theories are stuffed full of wild blueberry muffins. Tell 'em the only reason that makes *any* sense is this: *it seemed like a good idea at the time.*

Launch the Spanish Armada? Seemed like a good idea at the time.

Invent the wheel? Seemed like a good idea at the time.

Drift back in time to 165 Before the Common Era and find out how one day's oil burns for eight? Seemed like a good idea at the time. Because Barry R. Levin was a smartass!

It was all contained in the suit of lights.

All of time, and the ability to drift backward, all of it built into the refined mechanism the academics called a *driftsuit,* but which we "fugitives" called our suit of lights. Like a toreador's elegant costume, it was a glittering, gleaming, shining second-skin. All the circuits were built in, printed deep in the ceramic metal garment. It was a specially developed cermet, *pliable* ceramic metal, not like the armor worn by our astronauts mining the Asteroid Belt. Silver and reflective, crosstar flares at a million points of arm and torso and hooded skull.

We had learned, in this time of miracles, that matter and energy are interchangeable; and that a person can be broken down into energy waves; and those waves can be fired off into the timestream, toward the light. Time did, indeed, sweep backward, and one could drift backward, going ever toward that ultimate light that we feared to enter. Not because of superstition, but because we all understood on a level we could not explain, that the light was the start of it all, perhaps the Big Bang itself.

But we *could* go fugitive, drift back and back, even to the dawn of life on this planet. And we could return, but only to the moment we had left. We could not go forward, which was just as well. Literally, the information that was us could be fired out backward through the timestream as wave data.

And the miracle was that it was all contained in the suit of lights. Calibrate it on the wrist-cuff, thumb the "activate" readout that was coded to the DNA of only the three of us who were timedrifters, and no matter where we stood, we turned to smoke, turned to light, imploded into a scintillant point, and vanished, to be fired away, and to reassemble as ourselves at the shore of the Sea of Reeds as the Egyptians were drowned, in the garden of Gethsemane on the night of Jesus's betrayal, in the crowd as Chicago's Mayor Cermak was assassinated by a demented immigrant trying to get a shot at Franklin D. Roosevelt, in the right field bleachers as the '69 Mets won the World Series.

I thumbed the readout and saw only light, nothing but light, golden as a dream, eternal as a last breath, and I hurtled back toward the light that was *greater* than this light that filled me...

...and in a moment I stood in the year 165 Before the Common Era, within the burned gates of the Second Temple, on the Mount in Jerusalem. It was the 24th day of the Hebrew month *Kislev.* 165 B.C.E. The slaughtered dead of the Greco-Syrian army of Antiochus lay ten deep outside. The swordsmen of the Yovan, who had stabled pigs in the *Beis Ha Mikdosh,* even in the holiest of holies, who had defiled the sanctuary which housed the menorah, who had had sex on the stones of the sacred altar, and profaned those stones with urine and swine...they lay with new, crimson mouths opened in their necks, with iron protruding from their bellies and backs.

Ex-college boy from Chicago, timedrifter, fugitive. It had seemed like a good idea at the time. I never dreamed this kind of death could be...with bodies that had not been decently straightened for display in rectangular boxes...with hands that reached for the bodies that had once worn them. Faces without eyes.

I stood in the rubble of the most legendary structure in the history of my people, and realized this had not been, in any way, a good idea. Sick to my stomach, I started to thumb my wristcuff, to return *now* to the Project labs.

And I heard the scream.

And I turned my head.

And I saw the *Kohane,* who had been sent on ahead to assess the desecration—a son of Mattisyahu—I saw him flung backward and pinned to the floor of dirt and pig excrement, impaled by the spear of a Syrian pikeman who had been hiding in the shadows. Deserter of the citadel's garrison, a coward hiding in the shadows. And as he strode forward to finish the death of the writhing priest, I charged, grabbed up one of the desecrated stones of the altar and, as he turned to stare at me, frozen in an instant at the sight of this creature of light bearing down on him…I raised the jagged rock and crushed his face to pulp.

Dying, the *Kohane* looked upon me with wonder. He murmured prayers and my suit of lights shone in his eyes. I spoke to him in Greek, but he could not understand me. And then in Latin, both formal and vulgate, but his whispered responses were incomprehensible to me. *I could not speak his language!*

I tried Parthian, Samarian, Median, Cuthian, even Chaldean and Sumerian…but he faded slowly, only staring up at me in dying wonder. Then I understood one word of his lamentation, and I summoned up the hypnosleep learning that applied. I spoke to him in Aramaic of the Hasmonean brotherhood. And I begged him to tell me where the flasks of oil were kept. But there were none. He had brought nothing with him, in advance of his priest brothers and the return of Shimon from his battle with the citadel garrison.

It was a time of miracles, and I knew what to do.

I thumbed the readout on my wrist-cuff and watched as my light became a mere pinpoint in his dying eyes.

I went back to Chicago. This was wrong, I knew this was wrong: timedrifters are forbidden to alter the past. The three of us who were trained to go fugitive, we understood above all else… *change nothing, alter nothing,* or risk a tainted future. I knew what I was doing was wrong.

But, oh, it seemed like a good idea at the time.

I went to Rosenbloom's, still in business on Devon Avenue, still in Rogers Park, even this well into the 21st century. I had to buy some trustworthy oil.

I told the little balding clerk I wanted virgin olive oil so pure it could be used in the holiest of ceremonies. He said, "How holy does it have to be for Hanukkah in Chicago?" I told him it was going to be used in Israel. He laughed. "All oil today is *'tomei'*—you know what that is?" I said no, I didn't. (Because, you see, I *didn't* say, I'm not a Good Jew, and I don't know such things.) He said, "It means impure. And you know what *virgin* means! It means every olive was squeezed, but only the first drop was used." I asked him if the oil he sold was acceptable. He said, "Absolutely." I knew how much I needed, I'd read the piece on Hanukkah history. Half a log, the Talmud had said. Two *riv-ee-eas.* I had to look it up: about eight ounces, the equivalent of a pony bottle of Budweiser. He sold it to me in a bottle of dark brown, opaque glass.

And I took the oil to one of the one hundred and sixty-three Gentiles on Project Timedrift, a chemist named Bethany Sherward, and I asked her to perform a small miracle. She said, "Matty, this is hardly a miracle you're asking for. You know the alleged 'burning bush' that spoke to Moses? They still exist. Burning bushes. In the Sinai, Saudi Arabia, Iraq. Mostly over the oil fields. They just burn and burn and..."

While she did what she had to do, I went fugitive and found myself, a creature of light once again, in the *Beis Ha Mikdosh,* in the fragile hours after midnight, in the Hebrew month of *Cheshvan,* in the year 125 B.C.E.; and I stole a cruse of oil and took it back to

⁎

Chicago and poured it into a sink and realized what an idiot I'd been. I needn't have gone to Rosenbloom's. I could have used *this* oil, which was pure. But it was too late now. There was a lot we all had to learn about traveling in time.

I got the altered oil from Bethany Sherward, and when I hefted the small container I almost felt as if I could detect a heaviness that had not been there before. This oil was denser than ordinary olive oil, virgin or otherwise.

I poured the new oil into the cruse. It sloshed at the bottom of the vessel. This was a dark red, rough-surfaced clay jar, tapering almost into the shape of the traditional Roman amphora, but it had a narrow base, and a fitted lid without a stopper. It now contained enough oil for exactly one day, half a log. I returned to the Timedrift lab, put on the suit of lights—it was wonderful to have only one of three triple-A clearances—and set myself to return to the Temple of the Mount, five minutes earlier than I'd appeared the first time. I didn't know if I'd see myself coalesce into existence five minutes later, but I *did* know that I could save the *Kohane's* life.

I went toward the light. I *became* a creature of the light yet again, and found myself standing inside the gates once more. I started inside the Great Temple...

And heard the scream.

Time had adjusted itself. He was falling backward, the spear having ripped open his chest. I charged the Syrian, hit him with the cruse of oil, knocked him to the dirt, and crushed his windpipe with one full force stomp of my booted foot.

I stood staring down at him for perhaps a minute. I had killed a man. With hardly the effort I would have expended to wipe sweat from my face, I had smashed the life out of him. I started to shake, and then I heard myself whimper. And then I made a stop to it. I had come here to do a thing, and I knew it would now be done because...nowhere in sight did *another* creature of shimmering light appear. We had much to learn about traveling in time.

I went to the priest where he lay in his dirt-caked blood, and I raised his head. He stared at me in wonder, as he had the first time.

"Who are you!" he asked, coughing blood.

"Matty Simon," I said. It seemed like a good idea at the time.

He smiled. "Mattisyahu's son, Shimon?"

I started to say no, Matty, not Mattisyahu; Simon, not Shimon. But I didn't say that. I had thought *he* was one of the sons, but I was wrong. Had I been a more knowledgeable Jew, I would have known: he wasn't the *Kohane Gadol.* He was a Levite from Moses's tribe; one of the priestly class; sent ahead as point man for the redemption of the Temple; like Seabees sent in ahead of an invasion to clear out trees and clean up the area. But now he would die, and not do the job.

"Put your seal on this cruse," I said. "Did the *Kohane Gadol* give you that authority, can you do that?"

He looked at the clay vessel, and even in his overwhelming pain he was frightened and repelled by the command I had made. "No...I cannot..."

I held him by the shoulders with as much force as I could

muster, and I looked into his eyes and I found a voice I'd never known was in me, and I demanded, *"Can you do this?"*

He nodded slightly, in terror and awe, and he hesitated a moment and then asked, "Who are you? Are you a Messenger of God?" I was all light, brighter than the sun, and holding him in my arms.

"Yes," I lied. "Yes, I am a Messenger of God. Let me help you seal the flask."

That he did. He did what was forbidden, what was not possible, what he should not have done. He put the seal of pure oil on the vessel containing half a log, two *riv-ee-eas*, of long-chain hydrocarbon oil from a place that did not even exist yet in the world, oil from a time unborn, from the future. The longer the chain, the greater the binding energy. The greater the binding energy, the longer it would burn. One day's oil, from the future; one day's oil that would burn brightly for eight days.

He died in my arms, smiling up into the face of God's Messenger. He went toward the light, a prayer on his lips.

Today, at lunch in the Commissary, Barry R. Levin slapped his tray down on the table across from me, slid into the seat, and said, "Well, Mr. Pretend Jew, tomorrow is Hanukkah. Are you ready to light the candles?"

"Beat it, Levin."

"Would you like me to render the prayers phonetically for you?"

"Get away from me, Levin, or I'll lay you out. I'm in no mood for your scab-picking today."

"Hard night, Mr. Simon?"

"You'll never know." I gave him the look that said *get in the wind, you pain in the ass.* He stood up, lifted his tray, took a step, then turned back to me.

"You're a Bad Jew, remember that."

I shook my head ruefully and couldn't hold back the mean little laugh.

"Yeah, right. I'm a Bad Jew. I'm also the Messenger of God."

He just looked at me. Not a clue why I'd said that. All scores evened, I didn't have the heart to tell him...

It just seemed like a helluva good idea at the time. The time of miracles.

Oil and Water

By Dani Shapiro

WHEN I WAS GROWING UP, WE NEVER VISITED MY FATHER'S
sister, my Aunt Shirl, who lived in Boston. The very mention of
her would cause my mother's eyes to cross. I knew that my mother
couldn't bear to be around her, although I didn't know why. The
few times I had been with Shirl, she seemed lovely. She had a
heart-shaped face framed by a widow's peak, and a musical voice
that always sounded slightly amused. Besides, she was my father's
younger sister, and I could see that he loved her. It's hard to pinpoint when, exactly, my mother and Shirl stopped speaking, but
I sensed with a child's intuition that whatever had happened
between them was deep and irresolvable.

Over the years, there were blow-ups. After returning from
my grandfather's Orthodox Jewish funeral, my mother, upset by
the starkness of the service, looked at her grieving sister-in-law

and called the ritual barbaric. Shirl didn't attend my Bat Mitzvah because she had the flu. But my mother decided Shirl looked down her nose at us because we weren't religious enough. My mother retaliated. She refused to attend one of Shirl's son's weddings. Instead she dressed me, for this black-tie affair, in a gingham dress, and sent me with my father. Shirl saw that as a slap in the face.

Gradually, these slights built a wall higher than it seemed any of us could cross. I never knew my cousins, and that made me, as an only child, even lonelier. Shirl and her family faded into the background of our lives until they seemed practically not to exist. I carried their loss around with me in the worst possible way, without even knowing it was there.

When I was twenty-three, my parents were in a car crash. My mother broke eighty bones. My father died. In the months that followed, whatever Band-Aids had held the family together were torn off completely. The rift between my mother and Shirl descended into true bitterness. A year later, when it was time for the ritual unveiling of my father's tombstone, Shirl was banned from the ceremony by my mother. "Your father would not have wanted her there," my mother said.

I remember standing on a cold November day at my father's grave site, the wind whipping my coat around my shins, and feeling the gnawing hole left inside me by his death was made even more ragged by the loss of my aunt—my father's sister. I couldn't imagine that she and I could ever be like family again. Not after all that bad blood.

But I had underestimated my Aunt Shirl. In the years after my father's death, she kept reaching out a hand to me. She called me each year on the anniversary of my parents' accident—the only relative to do so—and left messages on my answering machine, just to say she was thinking about me and knew how hard it was. At first, I wasn't able to reach a hand back. I felt my loyalty had to be to my mother. But the hole inside me that had been there since childhood, making me feel half-orphaned, finally became more than I could bear. I began to sneak off to see my father's sister in Boston, hiding the relationship from my mother. I knew my father had done the same thing—meeting her for lunch or dinner—never telling my mother.

Shirl has a beautiful old house, on a street lined with two-hundred-year-old beech trees. Her home is always cool and dark no matter what the season. To enter it is to enter another time. It is so quiet inside that you can hear all the clocks ticking. She always seems to have an assortment of homemade cookies ready, and never has a hair out of place. I find it easier to breathe when I'm with Shirl, as if her presence unplugs something deep inside my chest. We sit in the study, a wood-paneled room lined with leather-bound Hebrew books. Family photographs in silver frames are arranged on a desk. In front are color pictures of my father and my uncle Harvey, Shirl's brothers, men who died too young.

It's Hanukkah, and the winter light falls across the sofa where Shirl sits, holding a cup of tea in a hand that looks too young to be seventy. "Have I ever told you my rag man story?" she asks. She hasn't, but that doesn't matter. I'd listen to any of her stories over and over again, picking up details I hadn't heard before as if seeing new colors in a rich and intricate tapestry, one I have longed to feel and touch all my life.

"I was five and a half," Aunt Shirl began. "We lived on Central Park West, on the second floor. It was just before Hanukkah, on a bitter cold day, and my mother took me to Columbus Avenue to buy candles for the menorah. She promised to get me a cookie. The Upper West Side was a quiet neighborhood then. You could walk down a side street and not see a soul. Columbus Avenue had just a few shopkeepers and a Kosher butcher.

"There were brownstones along the street, and patio areas two steps down where there were big garbage cans. As we walked past one of them, my mother saw an old Jew. His beard was gray, he was covered with grime. He hadn't seen comfort in quite a while. He was a good-sized man.

"My mother said to him, 'What are you doing?' He said to her, 'This is how I make my living.' He had a stick with a nail on the end, and he was picking through rubbish barrels looking for rags. My mother told him, 'It's very cold out. Would you like some soup?' He shrugged his shoulders, and my mother said, 'Come with me.' I was just a child," Shirl laughs. "All I thought was, 'there goes my cookie.'

"When we got to our building, my mother told him we were Orthodox, and she would prepare something dairy for him to eat. In the meantime, wouldn't he like to take a hot shower and refresh himself? While he was in my parents' bathroom, my

✴

mother took away all his clothes. Then she laid out some of my father's clothes, and put money in the pockets. And when this man came out, he had a snow-white beard, and piercing, marine-blue eyes, with light in them. A beautiful face. He sat down, and my mother gave him some soup. The Hanukkah menorah was near us, on the windowsill, polished to a high gleam and ready for *yontef.* When the man was finished eating, he turned to my mother and asked, 'With what may I ask the almighty to bless you when I pray?'

"My mother said, 'I have everything. God has been good to us. I have two beautiful children.' She did not tell the man that she had tried to have another child, but had had several miscarriages. She was told she had a tumor. She could never have any more children.

"The man prayed," said Aunt Shirl, "and then he walked away. A few weeks later, after Hanukkah was over, my mother went to the doctor. After he examined her, the doctor said, 'Mrs. Shapiro, I am not a religious man, and I don't believe in miracles, but you are pregnant.'

"The baby was your uncle Harvey," Shirl says, her voice cracking as she glances at the photograph of her younger brother, a handsome, bearded man, middle-aged in the photo, now dead of a heart attack. I know she is thinking that, in our family, there have been too many early deaths, too much loss. And I can see that loss, welling in her eyes.

"When Harvey was born," she went on, "my mother had a difficult time. She was thirty-four, old for childbirth in those days. He was a very big baby, and he was breech. My father was terrified. It was the only time I can ever remember him crying. My mother told him not to worry. She had a sense that God meant for her to have this baby, and that nothing bad was going to happen."

Shirl finishes her story, and I sink back into my chair, fighting back tears. The Hanukkahs of my childhood seem far away, as if they happened in a different galaxy. There was always something missing, something I couldn't put my finger on. I can remember the menorah, reflected against the wintry darkness of the bay window in my parents' living room, and the little mesh bags of chocolate Hanukkah gelt, and the plastic dreidels I would spin and spin, alone on the floor. I received eight gifts during the holiday, a gift for every candle. Usually there was one big gift, like a basketball hoop for the backyard, and then lots of small ones, like mittens and socks. But Shirl's story seems to be about a truer kind of gift: the gift of believing in miracles. And by telling it, she is giving a miracle to me.

"Our love is such a gift," she tells me. "Who would have thought we'd be able to sit together like this? After everything that's happened?" Both of our eyes fill with tears, and the true lesson of Hanukkah is here to be learned in this quiet room, filled with the books and portraits of my ancestors. If my grandmother hadn't stopped the rag man on that snowy street sixty-five years ago, would my Uncle Harvey ever have been born? Is that the miracle? Perhaps, but I'm not sure.

It seems to me that the true miracle is that an elegant woman with a big heart, walking with her little girl on a Hanukkah errand, gave a man the gift of his own dignity. And that the little girl who witnessed that act grew up to be a gracious woman, gracious enough to reach across the wide, deep ravine of our family's bitterness and misunderstanding, and hold out a hand to me.

✳

Hanukkah in Malaga

By Peter S. Beagle

IT HAPPENED IN ANOTHER WORLD, A LONG TIME AGO. I
was twenty years old, newly graduated from college—by the grade-
skipping grace of the New York State school system—and wandering
Europe for no reason except that I was a writer, and Europe was
where American writers always went. I wonder whether that's still
compulsory, in an age where Hemingway, Fitzgerald, Stein and
Toklas and Paris in the 1920s are all receding so fast in our
cultural rear-view mirror. I'm told that it's Prague now, or maybe
that was last year. Kathmandu's been and gone. I know that.

My closest cousins are half-Mexican, and the elder of the two
was then married to a Spanish painter with relatives of his own in
Malaga, on the Mediterranean coast. He urged me to visit them—
the family name was Arroyo—and since I spoke some Spanish, by
virtue of my cousins, and a Malaga winter surely had to be warmer

than the one I was huddling through in Paris. I wrote a letter and caught a train without waiting for an answer. I remember that the journey over the Pyrenees took a day and a night, and that my compartment was full of cheerful young Spanish soldiers. One of them fell asleep on my shoulder.

I had hardly checked into the little pensione where I had rented a room when Diego showed up. Diego was the oldest son of the Arroyo family: short and bouncy, with permanently disheveled hair and a smile like morning. He talked very fast, always in the present tense, with the Andalusian accent that drops all internal "s" sounds, so that a word like *gustar*—to enjoy—turned in to *gu'tar* and *vestido*, clothing, became *ve'tido*. I don't think I caught one word in ten then, but it didn't matter. Diego had come to take me home.

Home seemed far too small an apartment for all the assorted Arroyos gathered there to welcome the American cousin. The fact that there was no actual blood connection between us meant absolutely nothing: Family was family. In the same way it took me some while to sort out Don Segundo Arroyo, his wife Dona Elvira, and their four children—Luisa, Fernando, and Josefina, along with Diego—from the relations, neighbors, and friends for whom there was never any exact translatable category, and who were likely to drop by without notice at, literally, any hour. The Arroyos weren't simply part of their community—they were a community. That winter in Malaga, they became my center of gravity.

All the Arroyos worked, except Josefina—*la sabia,* as she was called, the little wise one—who was still in school. Don Segundo was employed by the railroad, Diego and Fernando by a trucking company. Luisa, the oldest child, was at the time the only telephone operator in the nearby fishing village of Torremolinos, which was just then in the process of being discovered by people like Burt Lancaster and Ava Gardner. Every morning, her *novio*, Enrique, would arrive on his motorcycle to take her to work, riding pillion with her hair tucked away under a scarf and her mother's lunch in a bag under her arm. Whenever I read about that booming resort town Torremolinos now, I think of Luisa, and I wonder how many operators they must have there these days.

The Arroyos as a group were handsome and noisy—always excepting shy little Josefina—running to bold, slightly heavy features, striking gray-green eyes, and solid, strong country bodies. They were devout Catholics who utterly despised the clergy, not to mention the dictator Francisco Franco and his Mickey Mouse–hat-wearing *Guardia Civil.* Franco's grip on Spain was already slackening somewhat in those times, and the *Guardia* always patrolled in pairs, knowing themselves forever hated by all sides; but I was still astonished to hear Don Segundo or Diego roaring treason as we strolled along a crowded downtown street, always ending with *"Y no podemos hablar!"* which means "And we can't even talk!" If anybody ever stopped the Arroyos from talking about anything, I never heard about it.

They invited me with them everywhere: on picnics and fishing trips, to street fairs, *ferias,* to gatherings at friends' houses— and, of course, to bullfights. I went to one, and never to another; but the Arroyos hadn't read Hemingway, and didn't hold my

American squeamishness against me. Fernando and his fiancée, Claudia, took me, along with Luisa and Enrique. There was another woman too, whose name I don't remember. It took me that whole afternoon to realize at last that she was Enrique's bad girl, acknowledged but never accepted: an implicit masculine necessity until he and Luisa were married. When we left the arena, she walked behind us, weeping silently. I dropped back and tried to talk with her, but either my Spanish wasn't good enough, or my understanding. The Arroyos—truly good, truly humane people that they were—never said a word about her.

Hanukkah has never been a major Jewish holiday in any country but the United States, where immigrant families realized quickly enough that their children were going to need some small counter weight to Christmas. In my unobservant home, my mother cooked potato pancakes, latkes; we lit the menorah candles every night of the eight-night celebration (my younger brother and I always squabbled over whose turn it was), and we sang the ancient Hanukkah blessing over them. But that was about it. We never exchanged more than token gifts, unlike a lot of the Jewish kids in the neighborhood, who scored twice each December. It was fun, and warming, but it wasn't a big deal.

But I'd always been home for Hanukkah before, even during my college years. This year I wasn't, and I knew inside myself that I never really would be home again. And it ached, which surprised me, unbeliever that I've always been. I don't know how I showed it—stoicism is far more deeply rooted than Hanukkah in my family's traditions—but Dona Elvira cornered me one afternoon and asked me bluntly, *"Que pasa con ti? Porque esos larmas sin llorar?"* What's the matter with you? Why these tears without crying? Dona Elvira spent most of her days in the kitchen, but she knew stuff.

I can't remember now what I answered, or how long it took Dona Elvira to get the truth out of me. But she got it, and she spoke of it to Don Segundo and the children, and they set out to give me a Hanukkah.

This was more than usually difficult for them. They had a coming Christmas on their hands (and a Spanish Christmas is a full-time, all-consuming job), and they knew less about Hanukkah than they did about Keynesian economics. But they were clear on candles—between religious festivals and the unreliable electric system, candles the Arroyos had. Menorahs were another matter: they knew no Jews, nor any shop in Malaga that might have stocked Jewish ritual objects. But Diego did have a friend apprenticed to a commercial potter, and the friend, on his own time, somehow produced a genuine clay menorah. It looked remarkably like a baseball glove, and it rocked precariously on its round base; but it had the required eight sockets, and one extra for the shammes, the candle that lights the others. But there's nothing in the Talmud governing the shape of menorahs. Nothing matters but the light.

Dona Elvira made the latkes. She was a splendid cook in the normal way, but her latkes were splendidly dreadful: doughy and lumpy as old mattresses—tasting like them too, for the matter of that. But she peered into my face with pride and anxiety as she served them to me—garnished with orange slices, as I recall—and I ate every damn one. And loved them. And love them now.

And I not only sang the blessing my mother had taught me, as the Arroyos listened in honest fascination, but a barely remembered Hebrew song telling the story of the Jews reclaiming the desecrated temple at Jerusalem, and of the one small cruse of holy oil that miraculously burned for eight days of celebration. The Arroyos hardly understood a word of my halting translation, but they smiled and nodded, and patted my shoulders gently, and their eyes shone in the flickering light of that trembly homemade menorah. Catholics they might have been, but they knew how to treat family.

I have never written about that Malaga Hanukkah until now. I have never forgotten it.

Gifts of the Last Night

By Rebecca Goldstein

THAT THE WINDS HAD TAKEN POSSESSION OF MANHATTAN on this night of Hanukkah; that they were roaming the wide avenues, snarling and hissing like a pack of demons unloosed from Gehenna: this was not the way *she* would ever have described the situation. Pearl Pinsky had little use for metaphor and none at all for Old World hocus-pocus.

The simple facts: It was late December, early dusk, and cold. Damned cold. Devilishly cold. Those winds.

Pearl had been waiting for almost an hour at her bus stop, not far from Columbia University. Classes were suspended for the winter recess, and the neighborhood felt eerily emptied. She stood at this corner all by herself, as the savage evening deepened around her into demented night. Her eyes, streaming cruelly from the cold behind her bifocals, were the lone eyes focusing on the dimming west, from where she expected momentarily to see those bright headbeams, rounding the corner from Riverside Drive.

Meanwhile, it only got darker, and the imps of the air were whooping it up with the ends of the long woolen scarf Pearl was vainly attempting to keep wound across her face, breathing open-mouthed into the fuzzy wool to generate some warmth. It was an incongruous scarf to be seen on a middle-aged woman of an otherwise serious cast. Splattered with primary colors, it was like something a little child might have worn, or perhaps even have painted. So that he knew at first glance this was a woman who gave little thought to appearances. However, whether this was the fault of her personality or her politics, this he couldn't have said, at least not from the first glance.

So then, who is this *he,* who is now all of the sudden coming in with a glance—knowing this, not knowing that, and in general confusing the reader? He happens to be someone who has a lot to say about how this story is told, and one thing is for sure: He doesn't like confusion in his stories. So let us fill in and make clear.

Beyond the point at which Pearl had given up all hope of seeing her bus on this given night; at exactly the point at which she had even despaired of finding a taxi on this lonely stretch of Broadway abandoned of godless guests; at just that moment she turned and noticed a little plain restaurant. Nothing fancy, nothing trendy. To say it was modest is already to overdo it. Not a glance of the brilliance of the festive season fell upon it. Not a single

✳

colored light bulb glimmered, not a glitter of a word had been
hung to wish a patron or a passerby a merry this or a happy the
other. Squeezed in as it was, between the corner and a dazzlingly
done-up Gap store, glowing with a white star and a sentimental
message, a person might almost not have noticed it at all, but
Pearl had noticed. The winds themselves had taken hold and
almost lifted her bodily from the pavement—she was after all not
so much to lift, a short woman, full-figured, but still not weigh-
ing more than maybe 115 pounds—and had urgently nudged her
through the door, slamming it shut behind her, so that again all
was calm within the ill-lit establishment, where a lone customer
sat eating his applesauce.

He looked up, his spoon poised on its way to his open mouth,
and stared intently at the bedraggled female suddenly brought
before his gaze. The intellectual high forehead; black-framed
glasses and slightly sagging jowls; the bulging book satchel,
incongruous scarf, and unraveling skirt drooping from beneath
her coat: He took note of all the telling details, but the scarf most
of all. He was a writer.

Meanwhile, as the writer was avidly scrutinizing, Pearl Pinsky
was seeing nothing at all. The overheated air of the restaurant
hitting the frozen lenses of her bifocals had completely misted
them over. She took them off and began to rub them vigorously
with one end of her woolen scarf, taking care to do a thorough job
of it, since she hated for obscurity of any sort to come between
her and the world. So the writer had a few long minutes to make
his observations and hazard his deduction.

Her age he guessed exactly. It was what she looked, and a woman who wore such a scarf would have taken no pains to disguise the truth.

Years ago, when the writer had been a man in all his vigor, he used to feel a certain mild outrage with such a woman as this, who took so little care to acknowledge and augment the feminine principle within her. This had been a great theme for him, both in his work and in his life: namely, the feminine principle. With him, it had never simply been a matter of a love affair, of which he had had a not insignificant number. Rather it had been more a matter of paying homage to the feminine principle, wherever he had happened to find it realized, and available, in this or that particular lady of his acquaintance.

He had been born to a woman who had known, even while he had not yet vacated her womb, that her firstborn would be a boy-child of remarkable genius, destined to transform, at the least, the century. Nothing in his childhood had dimmed his mother's certainty, which had, quite naturally, been duplicated in his. The consequence was that he had been the sort of a man who couldn't feel the insistent urgings of his manhood without at the same time endowing them with universal themes and erecting them into a theory of art and of life.

The exact details of this theory we can forget, because even the writer had by now forgotten them. They had gone the way of the urgings. So that now he could examine this woman, still busy with her bifocals, and take in the telling details with nothing of his old outrage.

✳

All evening long he had been aquiver with anticipation, since tonight was the very last night of Hanukkah, and he could not suppress his sense that the universe was not altogether indifferent. It had been the tradition, when he had been a boy, that each successive night of Hanukkah, his presents from his parents had gotten progressively more wonderful, a practice grounded in sound theology. After all, the ancient miracle of the little holy lamp that had continued to burn on such meager fuel: This miracle had gotten better and better with each passing day.

He couldn't remember now whether his sisters, too, had received gifts of mounting extravagance. His parents had been hard-working immigrants, their circumstances cramped. Maybe the sisters had received joint presents, as would have suited what had seemed to be their joint existence. He, the supremely only son, had simply thought of the three—Ida, Sophie, and Dorothy—as "the sisters."

But the presents that it had been his to receive on those last nights of the magical Hanukkahs of his childhood: these he could recall in loving detail to this day. When he had been five years old, he had received a tiny violin, sized just right for his little cheek and shoulder. When he had been six, it had been the entire set of the *Book of Knowledge* encyclopedias, all of whose twenty-five volumes, with appendix, he had read by the time he was eight. In fact, it had been of his beloved *Book of Knowledge*, with its many magnificent pages of full-colored plates, that he had only now been thinking when the restaurant door was flung open, and his attention diverted. So that when Pearl

Pinsky finally returned her defogged bifocals to the bridge of her nose—not a bad nose, he had noted, though a little wide—she found an old man's watery, red-rimmed eyes avidly fixed upon her.

By this time the writer knew what he knew, and he closed his mouth around a smile as if he and this woman were on old familiar terms with one another.

"Do I know you?" asked Pearl.

"Such winds," responded the writer, with a sympathetic little shiver. "Snarling and hissing like a pack of demons unloosed from Gehenna."

"Gehenna!" the woman gave a short little hoot of a laugh. She had a high-pitched voice, more girlishly sweet than he would have anticipated, with just a hint of the plaintive to curdle it. Without any ceremony, she came over and sat herself down opposite the writer at his little Formica table against the wall. "Gehenna!" she repeated as she placed her bookbag on the floor between her feet. Her purse she continued to hold, cradling it beneath her arm. "I thought it was supposed to be hot in Gehenna!"

"You thought wrong," the writer answered, and at last he took the spoonful of applesauce into his mouth, his jaws slowly working as if he were chewing, though all the time he didn't take his eyes from the woman.

Pearl was inclined to hoot once again, but she only snorted, and rather gently at that. The man across from her—palsied and bent, with only his imperious nose and vivid eyes still undiminished—was about the same age that her own father would have been, although her father would have had even less use than she for the quaint choice in metaphor just voiced. Simon Pinsky had been all sorts of things in his lifetime, including the editor of a Jewish anarchist newspaper, which had had its heyday when Pearl had been a child. She and her anarchist father had been comrades till the end, and Pearl had always felt most comfortable with men of Simon's generation.

"You know, it's a funny thing," she confided, after she had given her order for tomato soup to the young waitress, who could barely be bothered, "I wait at the corner almost every evening for my bus, and I never once noticed this restaurant."

"You're probably preoccupied. You strike me as a very preoccupied person."

He stared at her for some moments more.

"I wonder," he began slowly, "I wonder if you even realize what tonight is."

She looked at him blankly.

"It's the eighth night of Hanukkah—the very last night—the best night!" He finished on a high note, almost a squeak. A spray of spittle punctuated his excitement.

"Well, you're right there," Pearl answered, frankly taken aback. The old man was leaning toward her, his striped tie in his applesauce, his eyes, protuberant to begin with, gazing into hers with strange meaning. "I mean you're right that I wasn't aware."

"I knew it! I knew you had forgotten!"

"It doesn't mean all that much to me."

"You think you have to tell me that. You think I can't figure that out for myself?" he demanded in an aggrieved tone. He sat back in a sulk.

"So why's the last night the best night?" Pearl asked him. Her father had also had a quirky temper, as had many of the men of his generation whom Pearl had known, so she was an old pro when it came to this kind of appeasement. "I never heard that one," she threw in for good measure.

He didn't want to admit to her that the source of his pronouncement was only the order in which he had received his Hanukkah presents as a boy. She was clearly a very intelligent woman. He wouldn't be surprised to learn that she was a lady professor. But still she was also, just as clearly, a person completely ignorant on the subject of Jewishness, so that he could lie to her if he wanted, which he did want.

"It's part of the religion," he said, and took another spoonful of his applesauce.

"So if this is the best night, you should at least have some potato latkes to go with that applesauce," she said, smiling so girlishly sweet that he immediately repented. It was a mean trick to mislead someone about religion.

"You know what, miss?"

"Pearl," said Pearl.

He reached into his pants pocket, fumbling around until he pulled out a little black book and handed it across the table to her. It was cheap imitation black leather, embossed with gold Hebrew letters.

"It's a Jewish calendar," he said, smiling with the sudden

pleasure of his own generosity. "Organizations are always sending them to me, whether I send them back a donation or not. This one happens to be the nicest, but I have others. Take it, it's hardly ever used. One or two appointments I had in September, I penciled them in, but I'm not so much in demand as I used to be. It's almost good as new, Pearl. And all the Jewish holidays they've got printed up, even the exact moment of the sunset when they start. This way you'll at least know when you're not observing."

"Well, thank you," Pearl said, her voice gone more girlish than ever. "Will you inscribe it for me?" she asked, a little shyly.

"With pleasure," he answered. He was, after all, a writer. It wasn't the first time in his life his autograph had been shyly requested. Women, young and old, married and single, used to flock when he had given readings, and then they would line up afterward to have him sign copies of his stories that they had clipped out from the Jewish newspapers.

Pearl began to fish around in her purse for something to write with, but he quickly produced his own beautiful silver fountain pen, a gift he had received many years ago from one of his wealthier girlfriends.

"Hanukkah, 19--," Pearl read. "With my best wishes on the last night—I.M. Feigenbaum." Pearl looked up, her intelligent high forehead creased into wondering disbelief, her bifocals slipping down to the very tip of her short, wide nose. "I.M. Feigenbaum? Are you *the* I.M. Feigenbaum? I.M. Feigenbaum, the writer?"

"You know me?" the writer whispered, barely able to control his quivering voice. "You know me?"

Did Pearl Pinsky know I.M. Feigenbaum? And how she knew I.M. Feigenbaum! His brief heyday had coincided with the brief heyday of her father's paper, and sometimes Simon would receive a manuscript of a short story from the young author. Pearl's father had *detested* the writer I.M. Feigenbaum. It was not simply that this upstart was a sentimental bourgeois, whose writing did not even acknowledge the great class struggles of the day. It was far worse. His stories wallowed in superstition and obscenity, unnatural lusts alternating with Old World hocus-pocus, and Simon Pinsky had regarded each and every page from the pen of I.M. Feigenbaum as a profound and personal insult.

"Don't defile our trash cans with it!" Simon Pinsky would command to his wife, who helped out with the editing. "Our garbage is too good to be associated with it! Flush it down the toilet, Hannah!"

Simon Pinsky, as radical as he had been in his politics, also had an almost rabbinical aversion to vulgarity. To hear him utter such a word as "toilet" was painful for his wife and daughter. (A secret: Hannah Pinsky, an otherwise dutiful wife, had saved each and every one of those rejected manuscripts.) In any case, such was the effect that the writer I.M. Feigenbaum used to have on Simon Pinsky.

Pearl's was a forthrightly truthful personality. When she knew something, her procedure was to come right out and say it. It was in her nature, therefore, to explain precisely how it was that she came so well to know the name of I.M. Feigenbaum.

But for once in her life, she held her tongue. Staring across the little Formica table at the trembling old man, whose face was luminous with the wonder of this extravagant gift, Pearl Pinsky blessedly held her tongue.

The Demon Foiled

By Anne Roiphe

THE NEW MAYOR OF THE CITY WAS JEWISH, WHICH DIDN'T mean he wouldn't celebrate Kwanza. Also Christmas Mass at the Cathedral of Our Lady of the Sea, which spread solid and squat across two blocks of prime downtown real estate. He would appear at the food kitchen serving the homeless a meal of turkey and cranberries, and sing along with a gospel choir. The camera would find him at a shelter for abused women, dressed as Santa Claus, some weeks before the actual birth date of the significant baby. He had been elected by a mere hair and was quite sure that many felt he was not up to the task, too inexperienced, too much an outsider, not a man of the people at all. He was aware that the schools were run down and the class size too large and the bridges in need of overhaul. For months now he had been worrying about bottom lines, the appearance of favoritism here or there, the failure of those he had appointed to stem the tide of disarray. He knew that taxi drivers might strike along with the elevator men and sanitation workers and at least half the libraries might have to close because the funds were not there. He knew that the prisons were so crowded that riots were imminent, but the citizens still felt unsafe in their neighborhoods, and that the police sometimes behaved like warlords and the minorities in his city did not trust the particular minority that had nurtured the mayor himself. All this gave him a headache, the kind that two aspirin hardly touched.

The mayor's wife had prepared for Hanukkah as she always did. The children and the children's children would come for supper. There would be presents for the younger children and then they would light the candles. This year they would do so for the cameras. His aides had thought it would be helpful to show the mayor to his fellow citizens as a man who respected his tradition, a man of God, a family man. The mayor's wife had purchased a larger, more elaborate, more silver menorah than they had ever had before. This one had an eight-inch Lion of Judah at the base and grape leaves and pomegranates engraved on the cups that would hold the blue and white candles. The mayor's grown daughter had placed red velvet ribbons in her own daughter's hair and had insisted her son wear his jacket. The mayor's son, who privately felt that his father was a bit old for the job and should have let a younger man take his place at the top of the ticket, shaved so thoroughly that he cut himself and arrived with his new baby and six-year-old twins at the mayor's house with a bit of bloody tissue pressed to his cheek. He reminded his twins not to say "Merry Christmas" to their grandparents. In silent pluralism lay unity was his policy.

This year the mayor's wife did not make the potato pancakes herself. The cook made them and burnt them and made a new batch. The children did not eat them because they did not like them, they never had, although each year the mayor's wife offered them. The cook had to make them pasta with butter instead. They also did not like gefilte fish, kugel, brisket, matzo balls, or apples with honey. So be it. They could always have pasta. The mayor wanted to tell the children how his mother had ground the pota-toes and added onions and fried them on her old stove and the smell clung to his clothes for days. But he had told them all that before. There was nothing new to say. For the cameras he had prepared a speech. He had rehearsed it as he dressed in the morning and added to it during the day in the seconds between appointments. He had thought of the ending in the five minutes before his luncheon guest, the CEO of a major firm that was thinking of moving offices out of town, and was angling for some tax concessions (also tickets to the opening game of the baseball season), had arrived. He had polished it while waiting for his internist who had dismissed his stomach ailments as occupational hazards and suggested a week in Florida, which could not and would not be fit into the schedule.

The computer games his wife had purchased for the children seemed to be accepted with pleasure but then one of them was lost in the pile of blue and white and silver paper on the floor. The new owner of the game wept and stamped his feet and the mayor's son had to fold each piece of paper before it was found. The baby whimpered and howled and would not be comforted. The room is too hot, said the mother of the infant. The windows were opened. It is too cold, said one of the twins, who wrapped herself in the mayor's wife's velvet evening coat. The stuffed mouse and the soft elephant were greeted with hugs but then forgotten behind the couch. The daughter and the son made polite conversation, but the mayor heard the ice cracking as they spoke. It had always been that way. Their conversation was strained through the sieve of years, through the small resentments and the larger ones that formed a toxic plume snaking its way across the living room rug. The mayor preferred to ignore these particular hostilities. The mayor of such a city knew all there was to know about the jockeying for personal advantage, the petty adversarial words of one for another, and wished with all his heart that he had not been persuaded to invite the press to his home for the lighting of the candles. But he had.

The time came. The party assembled around the now cleared dining table. The TV cameras moved in to show the glorious menorah. There was a moment of quiet and the mayor's wife said the prayer, which was not so short because it was the last night of Hanukkah, and the mayor's oldest grandson took the match to the large candle and lit it and then he lit all the candles, one after the other and the TV cameras rolled and the child's face in the candlelight glowed and his cheeks were pink and the picture was picture perfect and the mayor cleared his throat ready to give his speech

✳

when suddenly the candles that had been lit went out, one by one, just as they had been lit, each leaving behind a little wisp of smoke that curled upward toward the ceiling. It must be a draft, it must be the open window. "Cut, cut," said the mayor's aide to the TV cameramen who did not stop their cameras. The mayor's son picked up the matches and relit the candles, the mayor's wife said the prayer again, not sure if that was the right thing to do or not. The candles burned for a moment and then again, as if the wicks were made of river water, they sank into darkness. The mayor's daughter tried and the mayor's son-in-law tried and each time the candles flamed up and then died as if a great breath had blown on them. Everyone in the room turned toward the mayor. He would have to explain this. He would have to explain the failure of his menorah to light to all the citizens of the city who would see it on the evening news.

The mayor was mute. His eyes were frightened. He could find no words for this strange, unnatural occurrence. His wife had tears in her eyes. His daughter was sulking her terrible sulk. His son was not entirely dissatisfied. What was this? The mayor searched his mind. Was it a sin of his? Was it a sign that God had deserted his people? Was it a sign that he had gone too far in calling the Cardinal your excellence the week before? What had he done that his candles would not light?

Behind the drapery the Spawn of Lilith, the Demon of political turmoil, had waited, stamping his little feet and hugging himself in malicious delight. Now unseen by human eye he floated past the mayor, a tip of his scaled hoof brushing across the forehead of the now sweating mayor. There was noise in the room. The aides were trying to spin the situation, "a cold air, bad candles, damaged wicks, sabotage by the other party." Then the mayor raised his arms and he spoke. He understood the reverse miracle, which was itself a sort of miracle.

"This was a year for darkness," he said, "for the lights that would not light. This is a promising sign, a menorah in rebellion against taking things for granted," he said, "clearly this is a hint of good things to come, a positive miracle, because," said the mayor although this was not the speech he had rehearsed at all, "out of darkness creation began, out of the void there came a new beginning, and this darkness will be the beginning of all our people of our city living together not in a grim truce but in mutual respect and true affection one for another. The darkness of this menorah is the beginning of our new light. It is our opportunity to create a better world than the one we live in now. Take a moment everyone, respect the darkness cast by the non-lighting candles. Out of the void the beautiful world was once formed.

"These candles are not burning and in their not burning they leave us in darkness and this darkness tells us that light will surely return, spring will come, that men are brave and nations can defend themselves against evildoers. We are not afraid of the dark."

The Demon hearing those words knew he was defeated. Depressed, deflated he left the mayor's house disguised as an uneaten potato pancake. Before he departed he hid the computer games in the bag of a cameraman who would not find them until long after Easter.

The mayor shot so high in the polls that there was talk of his running for president. After all, someone has to be the first Jewish president.

A Hanukkah Story

By Elie Wiesel

I DREAM OF HANUKKAH AND I SEE SNOW, SNOW EVERYWHERE. It envelops the low houses and the turrets of the distant castle. And I see a little Jewish boy. His name is Shimele, the diminutive of Shimon, and he is twelve years old. He is coming from heder; it is the hour of twilight. It's the first evening of the Festival of Lights. The first candle awaits him. The little Jewish boy will look at the glowing candle vanquishing the inauspicious shadows. He loves these candles and the story they tell—a heroic and vibrant history of faith and truth that celebrates faithfulness. This is the festival of presents, the festival of children.

The street the little boy enters is deserted. Wrapped up warmly in his coat that weighs heavily on his frail shoulders, Shimele is in a hurry; yet he proceeds slowly for fear of slipping. He is careful but ends up falling. A voice in Romanian reaches him from a carriage entrance: "That's where you belong, you dirty Jew—on the ground."

The little boy repeatedly tries to get up but does not succeed. Every time he tries he finds himself outstretched on the icy snow, his body aching. At one particular moment, he feels his face become warm. He heaves a sigh of fear: Blood trickles down his nose and his mouth and there is no one to come to his aid. A wave of panic hits him. If he lies there much longer, he will die. He then shuts his eyes and begins to pray. He says: "Lord, today is the first day of Hanukkah; you have worked a *great* miracle for the Maccabees; make just a *little* one for me." He repeats the prayer several times and I believe he even shed a tear or two.

All of a sudden, a shiver runs through him; he senses a presence. He knows that he is no longer alone. He opens his eyelids and catches sight of a large, bearded laborer with big shoulders, a fierce face, and a wild air about him. Who could he be? An enemy? No, a friend. "Don't be afraid, my boy," says the stranger as he helps him get up. "Stop your crying. Don't show that dirty dog that a Jew like yourself is afraid of him. Come, I'll take you home. You are undoubtedly late, and your parents must be worried." The laborer takes Shimele by the arm and he feels light and safe; they fly to his house. The door opens by itself. Shimele wants to thank his rescuer, but the man is no longer there, as if the snow or the night had swallowed him whole.

Now the little Jewish boy recognizes that the laborer was right. At home, his parents are crazed with worry. Shimele's mother rushes out of the kitchen, returning with a wet towel to clean his face. "Shimele! You're hurt! And what happened to you, my poor child? You are covered with blood. Who hit you?" The little boy reassures her. He tells her what happened. The fall in the snow, the mocking laughter of the hooligan and his insults. The sudden apparition—the unknown rescuer. Shimele's mother wants to ask him more questions, but his father interrupts: "Hanukkah awaits us...the first candle..." The entire family goes to the window where the candles must be lit. It is important that the candles be seen by neighbors, passersby, indeed, the whole world. Shimele's father recites the proper blessings and everyone sings the songs which accompany the prayers. Before, it was always Judah the Maccabee whom the little boy saw in his imagination before the pure and beautiful flames. Tonight, it's his rescuer who occupies his thoughts. And the next night, as well. In fact, Shimele can think of nobody else. At school, it is not Jacob and his son Joseph who interest him; it is the unknown laborer. Shimele burns with desire to see him again. To thank him, to confide in him, to make friends with him, to love him. During this time, he began to tell himself the stranger was perhaps Judah the Maccabee himself. Only he could arise from nowhere to hunt the enemies of our people. Only he would come to the rescue of threatened Jewish children. Will Shimele find him again? If so, how will he catch up to him? Where to seek him? At the synagogue or the house of study? There are several, perhaps far too many. The one of the Hassidim of Sapinka and the one of the Hassidim of Borshe.

The one of the tailors and the one of the Holy Brotherhood who look after burials. And so many others. What Shimele needs one more time is a miracle. Just a little one would suffice for him, a sliver of a miracle would make him happy.

The seventh day of the festival arrives. Shimele and his father go the railway station to welcome the celebrated Rabbi Mendel of Wizhnitz, coming for a visit to the home of his cousin the Rabbi of Seret. A large crowd had already turned out. The illustrious visitor, an old man with a radiant face, clasps people's hands and greets his intimate followers, asking one about the health of his daughter; another about his personal affairs. The people are so happy to see him among them they start singing a Hassidic Hanukkah song. It helps them a little to attain ecstasy. Shimele thinks that one might imagine oneself in the *"shtibel"* where every word becomes a song and every song transforms into prayer and, for an instant, letting himself go, he forgets his rescuer. At that moment he notices him. In the background, absorbed with something else, the laborer grabs hold of a large sack and places it on his shoulder. Shimele breaks away from his father and the crowd, and runs toward the man, who, one week ago, saved his life. Too late, the man has disappeared into one of the nearby lanes. Shimele goes right and left, asking passersby if they had seen a man carrying a sack. They laugh in his face: "Is it a porter you're looking for? You'll find ten or twenty at the railway station." Indeed, the porters are over by the railway station. Shimele goes from one to the other, all are big and strong. Some are surly, others cheerful, but not one turns out to be Judah the Maccabee.

Shimele is sure of one thing: Judah lives in his hometown, disguised as a porter. He derives from this a feeling of pride and bliss. Of all the places in the Diaspora, the Jewish warrior of antiquity chose this little mountain town to live in. But what does he carry in his sack? Could he be like the prophet Elijah who, according to legend, wanders throughout exile gathering the sad stories of oppressed Jews? Troubled, tormented, Shimele does not shut his eyes that night. He would give all he had to meet Judah again, to tell him his dreams and fears. To point out to him the houses where the bullies lived who thirst for Jewish blood, so that he might punish them. If he were able to do so, Shimele would quit school to spend all his time at the railway station: His porter would eventually reveal himself. But Shimele cannot do this. His parents would not permit him. The place of a Jewish boy is at the heder, the yeshiva, and not with porters.

But Shimele was wrong to make himself worry. He will meet his rescuer the next day. Shimele's father, surrounded by the whole family, lit the eighth and final candle. For the last time they joyfully sang their thanks to the God of Israel, for having saved them from the cruel hands of Antiochus Epiphanes. They hastily swallowed their dinner and went to the inn where the Rabbi of Wizhnitz was staying. All his followers were in attendance. Everyone wanted to see the Master at the moment when he would light the eight oil lamps in honor of the festival. In a state of immersed meditation, the Rabbi recited the prayer, and everyone responded with an amen. He lit the first lamp, breathed slowly, and then lit the second. A heavy silence separated the lighting of the fourth from the fifth. Following the seventh, he stopped. Nobody dared move. Everyone knew the Rabbi's custom of inviting someone else to complete the task. It was his way of blessing an individual and offering him a year of joy and happiness. The Rabbi lifted up his countenance and walked before his disciples. Whom will he choose? The porter was standing far in the back, but the Rabbi marked him out and signaled for him to approach. The porter murmured several inaudible words as if to get away, but the Rabbi seemed to order him to come. Submitting, the porter lit the last lamp. And the flame shooting up was the highest and purest of all.

After the ceremony, the Rabbi and the porter retired into a private room. They stayed there until midnight. Nobody ever knew what they talked about. All that Shimele knows is that the porter vanished from the town on the following day.

Hanukkah in the Age of Guys & Dolls

By Mark Helprin

IN THE AGE OF *GUYS & DOLLS* MORE THAN HALF A CENTURY ago, when I looked up at subway turnstiles and did not know how to read, bookies seemed to infest the United States by the million. Although I had never seen one, or even a picture of one, my impression was that they were everywhere, like fire hydrants. And had one of these creatures, as elusive as narwhales, been able to look forward into my life, he might have bet heavily that in regard to Hanukkah, I would be a kind of Jewish Scrooge.

I detest holidays, even my own birthday, which (perhaps coincidentally) is a holiday in Italy. Although it should not be necessary to explain praiseworthy revulsions, I will. My family was the very model of nuclear fusion, in that, with us, there were no spaces

between the particles, and the friction was immense and unquan-
tifiable. Everything was spoken, argued, known, supported, and
shared. My father and I would go on ten-hour walks (my mother
could not come, because she took little tiny steps) and upon our
return we would still be disputing the single point of contention
with which we had started out. If one of us was doing something
and another was not, the one who was not busy would watch. We
followed insanely E.M. Forster's advice, "Only connect," and, God
knows, we were close.

At the other extreme, one of my friends, the Jewish Grover
Cleveland—he looked like Grover Cleveland—came from a family
that existed at such galactic distances the one from the other that
on the rare occasions they were together they had to wear name
tags. Had they been gentiles the children would have been bun-
dled off to boarding school before they could lift their heads, but
they weren't, and the parents left instead—mainly for the "Copa,"
but also for Paris, Buffalo, and Maui. The father was as remote as
a king, the mother drove a car with red seats, and the children
thought like orphans. But they made a point of being together on
holidays, even Christian holidays, because then this otherwise
dysfunctional family would pretend to the world and to themselves that they were what they were not. And gleefully and mali-
ciously they would criticize us, we who stuck together like epoxy,
for failing to put on the same show: "You mean, you won't be
together for Bulgarian Constitution Day?" So, for me, very early
on, holidays became synonymous with insincerity and the merely
robotic simulation of human emotions.

As I grew older I saw that often where there was no love, love was falsely proclaimed on one day only; that where there was no connection, it was acted out on one day only. My belief was and is that you honor your principles every day, embrace your family every day, live right every day, and love deeply every day, not just when the moon is blue.

Nor have I ever been fond of two great holiday pillars—the expression of regard and affection through the exchange of gifts (pace O. Henry), and the investment in certain foods of significance beyond what they can bear. My own experience with gifts has invariably left me dejected and depressed where they are, as so often is the case, pressed into service to bridge empty spaces, to serve as a substitute for attention not paid, sacrifice not made, and promises not kept. I want no objects from those I love but only their health, their happiness, and their presence.

By the same token, keep me away from rhapsodies about potato pancakes. An idolatrous focus on anything, not least food, can, like carbon monoxide, usurp the place of the real oxygen of existence. And when people make latkes, mispronouncing the "es" as lat-keys, they, their hair, clothes, houses, and cars can smell of rancid oil until spring. Better to work as a fajita chef: At least you get paid and you can eat what you cook without the sensation of swallowing half a ton of library paste.

It is almost universal that Jews give presents on Hanukkah solely because it is close to Christmas, but why not just convert to Christianity, which might be simpler than trying to reconcile a Jewish military holiday with eight days of tearing up wrapping paper that just might be imprinted with pictures of elves.

By now the bookies would be taking bets with heavy odds, and they wouldn't even know what happened when yet another friend, in the third grade—he looked like the Jewish John Maynard Keynes, although he was still two years from his first mustache—invited me to his house for Hanukkah. I was terrified, but I was at least occupied with a task, for he had told me that he was going to give me the greatest present ever given. "Wait 'til you see it!" he would shriek. "No one in the world has ever gotten such a present!" This he elaborated every day for a month. "If God could make a present half as good, he would have made the earth." The heart of his campaign was the pronouncement, "Don't bother to get me anything special, don't even try, because you'll never in a million years be able to match what I'm going to give to you."

Thus manipulated, you might even say cornered, we bought him an aircraft carrier. Granted, it was not a real aircraft carrier, but it was the most magnificent model available, for a sum that with some augmentation would have sufficed to purchase a used automobile in very bad condition, say without an engine. I hauled it to his house, in its gift-wrapped box almost the size of a harpsichord, and sat down anxiously to dinner with his fierce and thuggish brothers, who were so vicious that, not long before, one of them had thrust a steak knife through the hand of another, pinning it to the table during the soup course. I had enough problems with Jewish holidays: I was not prepared for a reenactment of the crucifixion. And I was shy beyond measure. I wanted just to see the candles lit, eat my jelly doughnut, grab my splendid present, which I fervently hoped would be an aircraft carrier, and escape back to my house.

When he opened the aircraft carrier, which in the kid terms of the era was matchless, he was disappointed. "I like battleships better," he said, and stared at me as if expecting that I could build one on the spot. But his disappointment was bearable, because I knew that I could not equal what was coming. And, by the way, where was it? "I already gave it to you," he said.

"What?" I asked. "What did you give me?"

"The dreidel."

"The dreidel?" It was plastic, the size of my thumb, something that, if now there were six billion Jews in the world and fifteen million non-Jews instead of the other way around, you might get in a Cracker Jacks box.

"Isn't it *great*?" he asked. "Look! It's got a moving part. It *is* a moving part!"

The bookies of the era would have to have wagered that I would never appreciate this post-biblical festival of lights that most people believe cannot hold a candle to Christmas and yet by accident of birth is forced to try. But they and everyone else who simply plays the odds would have lost their bets.

Decades after my childhood, and yet decades ago, I lost control of my destiny and found myself in the Israeli army, an infantry-man on active service in Samaria on the West Bank of the Jordan, and on the border with Lebanon. My experience as a soldier occupying a conquered enemy territory reaffirmed for me the difficult coexistence of two basic truths—that the Palestinians had no intention of making peace and wanted Israel's destruction; and that Israel's continued occupation was both untenable and unjustifiable. The answer to this problem was the simultaneous creation of more defensible lines by Israel's annexation of higher ground to the west, and the emergence of a demilitarized Palestinian state in the population centers and fertile lands to the east. This was, more or less, the Allon Plan, which I supported, and which Allon supported. Unfortunately, that was about it.

When I realized this, I foresaw ineluctable suffering, bloodshed, misery, and death as clearly as one sees a storm approaching at sea. Caught between an implacable enemy and my own allies who showed both insufficient resolution and insufficient flexibility, I was inconsolable. Living each day with the prospect of endless war makes for a darkness that covers and obscures like a veil. The War of Attrition that fell into place after the temporary relief of 1967 served to remind Israel that it had been fighting for the whole century and might have to persevere in fighting for generation after generation.

In the dark at the beginning of the winter of 1972–73, I returned briefly to my kibbutz in the Beit Shan Valley, a place that in summer was not infrequently 120° F, but where now it was cold and clear. My leave was coincident with Hanukkah, which that year followed both the massacre in Munich and an autumn of fighting on the northern borders. Now the connection that had been clear to others came clear to me. Now, what had been hidden not only by my own insufficient education but by decades of accretion, imitation, prettification, and neglect, became apparent.

This is no pretty holiday of meaningless custom and empty ritual. More than two thousand years ago, the Jews fought a long and brutal war with the Syrians, who sought to Hellenize the Levant and to destroy Judaism altogether. For the Jews everything was at stake, from honor to existence, and they fought for year after year, until they achieved victory and the darkness of their struggle lifted. This, and the miracle of their perseverance as symbolized by the flame that burned when apparently it had no fuel, they commemorated by lighting lamps, which they put in the doorways of their houses, more than a century before the first Christmas.

There is no joy in military victory, or there should be none, because of the great cost. There is instead relief, gratitude, and an intensified appreciation of what we are given in so short a duration. And for soldiers and civilians in the darkness of war, this commemoration of victory past holds out the promise of survival and is a light that shines through.

On what I recall to have been a very cold night, we went out beyond the wire, and at a specified time lit a bonfire. And as we did, other fires were lit as well, both near and at great distances, across our valley, to the north, and at the tops of the rounded hills that are the mountains of Gilboa. Two thousand years later, we were still fighting in the same place, still struggling through veils of darkness, but we were still alive and we had the light of survival in our eyes.

As is the custom in Israel on this holiday, someone read from the Thirtieth Psalm: "Oh Lord...thou has lifted me up, and has not made my foes to rejoice over me...I cried unto thee, and thou hast healed me....Thou hast brought up my soul from the grave: thou hast kept me alive....For...weeping may endure for a night, but joy cometh in the morning."

Now that I have made my peace with Hanukkah, I see that it may not have been inappropriate that as a child I fought it. As a gift of a cold night three decades ago in the Beit Shan Valley, I see that I was in fact resisting everything but its essence. And this is what is right for all holidays, to resist and de-emphasize everything but their essence, so that if there is light in them it may shine through—and so that the bookies and anyone else who simply plays the odds may lose their bets.

The Miracle of the Oil

By Simone Zelitch

ONCE, IN THE AGE OF THE MACCABEES, THERE LIVED AN old Jew named Eleazar, who guarded the courtyard of the Holy Temple while a single flask of oil burned for eight days. Because he had stood watch while the miracle took place, there were some who believed he had taken on a little of its glory and a little of its light. After a while, in spite of his good sense, Eleazar began to believe it himself.

Then, one day, Eleazar had a visitor. A lamp-maker knocked on his door, and said, "I need to make peace with you, Eleazar. When I heard we only had one flask of oil for the rededication, I found a little in my shop, and I slipped past you into the sanctuary and fed the flame."

Eleazar was stunned. The fire burned in a holy place, and only the High Priest was permitted there. It stood to reason that the lamp-maker should have been struck dead. But clearly, he'd meant no harm. So Eleazar said, "The Lord works through plain and honest Jews like you. Go in peace."

So Eleazar made peace with the knowledge that God worked a wonder through an ordinary man. But then, one day, he had another visitor, a woman. Her hair was white, and her expression, haunted. Eleazar greeted her with courtesy, for she was Hannah, the heroine who'd lost her seven sons because they wouldn't bow down to a pagan god.

Hannah said, "Something lays on my heart and I must make peace with you, old Eleazar."

Eleazar said, "No one deserves peace more than you."

"Then I will speak," said Hannah. "When I heard there was only a single flask of oil for the rededication, I couldn't bear to think that the flame would go out. I had a flask I'd once used to comb through the hair of my seven sons. It was good oil, and now I had no need of it, so I slipped past you, Eleazar, and into the sanctuary."

Eleazar caught his breath. Women defiled a sacred place. It was as though the altar stones had once again been soaked in pig's blood. He couldn't control his anger or confusion, for Hannah was an honorable woman, for whom no tribute was too great. How could he condemn her? So he mastered himself and said, "Go in peace."

That night, Eleazar could not sleep. He wrapped himself in his shawl, thinking and praying, he did not hear his next visitor arrive.

It was a young man with a shaved chin, and clipped curls, who stood half-naked in the cold. Eleazar recoiled from the sight of him. He said "You're wise to come at night. If pious Jews found you here by daylight, you'd be dead."

With a nervous smile, the young man said, "I am a Jew."

"A Hellenized Jew," Eleazar said. "You've come from the gymnasium, where Greeks teach youths to turn their backs on God and worship their bodies. It was your kind who bleated out philosophy while the seven sons of Hannah were slaughtered before her eyes."

"I am still a Jew," said the young man. "I'm also Greek. Is that impossible?"

Bitterly, Eleazar said, "Oil and water don't mix."

"Don't they?" The young man cocked his head. "Funny, old Eleazar, that you should bring up oil. We have quite a bit of olive oil at the gymnasium. We oil our bodies to make them beautiful. And rumor came to us that you were short of oil. That should have meant nothing to me, yet somehow it did, and I brought that oil and fed the flame and kept the fire burning.

Eleazar said, "The Maccabees fought against the likes of you."

"Yet I am a Jew," the young man said again.

Eleazar could not speak. He took a long look at the young man's face and saw there pride, anger, remorse, and a deep need to be told he had a share in the Temple. After a moment, with great effort, he took the young man's hand. "Go in peace," he said. "You have a Jewish soul."

He wanted to say more, but before he'd gathered words enough, the youth had gone.

Eleazar could not sleep that night, pondering the oil poured by transgressors. Was he right to grant them peace? In the days of the Judges, they would have been condemned. In the days of the Prophets, they would have been chastised. Yet, Eleazar knew, there were no more Judges in Israel, and the age of Prophets had ended long ago. Now, Jews found God in each other, in acts of courage and in acts of kindness. God's arms are open. God forgives. God answers light with light.

Eleazar might have gone to sleep then, but someone else appeared at the door. "Old Eleazar!" The voice was thick, and the words slurred together. Eleazar did not return the greeting. "Old Eleazar," the visitor said again. "I'm come to make my peace with you."

"Take your peace and go," said Eleazar.

"I've come to tell you something. About the oil, old Eleazar."

"I know. It was a miracle," said Eleazar. "Now take your peace, friend, and go."

"You call me friend? But our people are deadly enemies. Do you grant friendship so easily?"

Then Eleazar looked up. In his doorway stood a man with shaggy hair and brilliant eyes. He wore a lion's skin and carried a tall, carved staff, and his teeth had been sharpened to points. Bracing himself, Eleazar said, "You are a Canaanite."

"I am," the man replied. "My people have lived in this city for thousands of years, when it was called Salem. Then you came, the people we call Habiru. On this mountain we had our temple of the Evening Star, and you made a ruin of it and massacred our people. Now, like us, you have been conquered. You rise up and call for freedom, and we join you, Eleazar. Our fates are bound together. And together we rededicated the Temple."

"You did not enter God's Temple," said Eleazar, and he turned away.

The Canaanite said, "We gave you oil, all we had."

"We took no oil from you," said Eleazar, and he turned back to his bed, hoping the Canaanite would pass like an evil dream.

"I stand before you, old man, at great peril of my life," the Canaanite said. "Would you sooner that there was no flame then, Eleazar. Would you sooner the flame went out?"

Eleazar pulled his shawl over his face. But the Canaanite did not go away. He waited for his answer.

About the Authors

MAX APPLE (b. 1941) is the author of *Roommates: My Grandfather's Story*, the biography of his immigrant grandfather, as well as the critically acclaimed short story collections *Free Agents* and *The Oranging of America*. Apple has an established career as a screenwriter, and his articles and stories have appeared in *Esquire*, the *New York Times*, the *Atlantic Monthly*, and other publications.

PETER S. BEAGLE (b. 1939), a World Fantasy Award nominee, is the bestselling author of the fantasy classic *The Last Unicorn* and many other acclaimed works, including the novels *The Innkeeper's Song* and *Tamsin*. His long career has included everything from journalism and stage adaptations to songwriting and performances.

ARIEL DORFMAN is a Chilean-American writer and human rights activist who holds the Walter Hines Page Chair at Duke University. His books, written both in Spanish and English, have been translated into more than thirty languages, and his plays staged in over 100 countries. Dorfman has received numerous international awards, including the Laurence Olivier Award. His novels include *Widows*, *Konfidenz*, and *Blake's Therapy*. He has just published a new novel, *Burning City*, with his son, Joaquin Dorfman.

DANIEL MARK EPSTEIN (b. 1948) is an award-winning poet and biographer whose works include *What Lips My Lips Have Kissed: The Loves and Love Poems of Edna St. Vincent Millay* and *Proust Regained*. His poetry has earned him numerous awards, notably an NEA Poetry Fellowship, a Guggenheim Fellowship, the Prix de Rome, and the Robert Frost Prize.

KINKY FRIEDMAN (b. 1944) was originally a country-and-western singer with the band Kinky Friedman and the Texas Jewboys, whose repertoire included "They Ain't Making Jews Like Jesus Anymore." Friedman went on to write a succession of crime thrillers, including *Ten Little New Yorkers* and *Elvis, Jesus and Coca-Cola*. In the spring of 2005 he announced his plans to run for Governor of Texas in 2006.

HARLAN ELLISON'S (b. 1934) writing career has spanned more than fifty years. He has written or edited more than seventy-five books as well as 1700-plus stories, essays, and articles. Ellison has been included in the annual Best American Short Stories and his classic fantasy, "'Repent, Harlequin!' Said the Ticktockman" is one of the ten most reprinted stories in the English language. Ellison also has a successful career as a screenwriter, and has won the Hugo, MWA Edgar Allan Poe, World Fantasy, Nebula, and Bram Stoker awards, among others.

MYRA GOLDBERG (b. 1943) is a member of the writing faculty at Sarah Lawrence College. She is the author of the novel *Rosalind: A Family Romance* and *Whistling*, a collection of stories. Goldberg is working on a mystery about a missing tablet from the Baghdad Museum.

REBECCA GOLDSTEIN (b. 1950) is a MacArthur Fellow and the author of five novels, including *The Mind-Body Problem* and *Properties of Light*, as well as one book of short stories, *Strange Attractors*. Her most recent book is *Incompleteness: The Proof and Paradox of Kurt Gödel*, an examination of the mathematician's life and work. Goldstein is a visiting professor of philosophy at Trinity College in Hartford, Connecticut.

MARK HELPRIN (b. 1947), educated at Harvard, Princeton, and Oxford, served in the Israeli Army, Israeli Air Force, and British Merchant Navy. He is the author of, among other titles, *A Dove of the East and Other Stories*, *Refiner's Fire*, *Ellis Island and Other Stories*, *Winter's Tale*, *A Soldier of the Great War*, *Memoir From Antproof Case*, and *Pacific and Other Stories*.

GLORIA DeVIDAS KIRCHHEIMER is the author of the story collection *Goodbye, Evil Eye*, a National Jewish Book Awards finalist, and coauthor, with Manfred Kirchheimer, of *We Were So Beloved: Autobiography of a German Jewish Community*. She has been published in literary magazines and widely anthologized. Under the name Gloria Levy she made one of the earliest recordings of Sephardic folk songs in the United States.

LESLÉA NEWMAN (b. 1955) is the author of more than fifty books, including *Heather Has Two Mommies*, *A Letter To Harvey Milk*, *Write From The Heart*, and *In Every Laugh a Tear*. She has received many literary awards, including poetry fellowships from the National Endowment for the Arts, the James Baldwin Award for Cultural Achievement, and three Pushcart Prize Nominations. Nine of her books have been Lambda Literary Award finalists.

DANIEL PINKWATER (b. 1941) is the author of more than eighty books, most for children and young adults, including *Lizard Music*, *The Hoboken Chicken Emergency*, and *The Artsy Smartsy Club*. He is a frequent commentator for National Public Radio's "All Things Considered" and "Weekend Edition Saturday."

ANNE ROIPHE (b. 1935) is the bestselling author of fourteen books, including the acclaimed *Fruitful: Living the Contradictions: A Real Mother in a Modern World*, which was on the shortlist for the National Book Award in 1996. She writes a biweekly column for the *New York Observer*, and her articles and criticism have appeared in *Vogue* and *Glamour*, among other national publications.

DANI SHAPIRO (b. 1962) is a novelist whose books include *Playing With Fire*, *Fugitive Blue*, *Picturing the Wreck*, and the bestselling memoir *Slow Motion*. Her latest novel, *Family History*, was published by Knopf in 2003. Shapiro teaches in the graduate writing program at The New School in New York City.

ELIE WIESEL (b. 1928) is a Holocaust survivor, a world-renowned author, and recipient of the Nobel Peace Prize. His most famous work, *Night*, is an account of his experience in Hitler's concentration camps. Wiesel is the Andrew W. Mellon Professor of Humanities at Boston University.

SIMONE ZELITCH (b. 1962) is the author of three novels, *The Confession of Jack Straw*, *Moses in Sinai*, and *Louisa*, which was the recipient of the Goldberg Prize. A former Peace Corps volunteer, she teaches at Community College of Philadelphia, and is completing a novel about Mississippi Freedom Summer.

THE HANUKKAH LIGHTS CD

The *Hanukkah Lights* CD features the original NPR broadcast recordings of Susan Stamberg and Murray Horwitz reading four additional Hanukkah stories.

1. *The Two Menorahs* by Daniel Mark Epstein
   On the first night of Hanukkah, two men engage in a lively discussion over the traditions of the menorah—and discover the healing power of argument.

2. *A Candle for Kerala* by Ariel Dorfman
   A lonely man finds love over the phone—long-distance, in India—when he tries to amend a Hanukkah Internet shopping disaster.

3. *A Hanukkah Story* by Kinky Friedman
   Kinky Friedman provides his typically off-center point of view when retelling the story of Hanukkah, introducing OPEC, Leonard Cohen, and the Electric Matzoball disco to the traditional tale.

4. *Hanukkah at Tiffany's* by Lesléa Newman
   When her precocious granddaughter rejects her traditional Jewish name in favor of "Tiffany," a wise Nana shares her own struggle with names.